The Hardy Boys®
in
Footprints Under the Window

The Hardy Boys Mystery Stories®

Footprints under the Window

Franklin W. Dixon

Armada

First published in the U.K. in 1972 by William Collins
Sons & Co. Ltd., London and Glasgow.
First published in Armada in 1976 by
Fontana Paperbacks,
8 Grafton Street, London W1X 3LA.

This impression 1984.

Printed in Great Britain by
William Collins Sons & Co. Ltd., Glasgow.

Frank, helpless in a choking grip, saw Chet thrown to the ground

CONTENTS

·1·

Shots Offshore

"FRANK—I've never seen so many guards at Micro-Eye before! And that steel wire fence is new. Think something is up?"

Blond, seventeen-year-old Joe Hardy, at the convertible's wheel, had stopped for a red light. His brother, dark-haired and a year older, peered out at Bayport's sprawling photographic plant.

"Must be a special project," Frank suggested.

The traffic light showed green and the Hardys' car moved past the block-long complex of buildings. Three uniformed guards were inspecting a departing Corporated Laundries truck at the gate.

Frank whistled. "Micro-Eye must be working on something that's top secret," he said. "I wonder if Dad knew about it before he left—" Frank broke off as the boys approached the rear of the main plant. A man was crouching on the outside of the fence. He was trying to cut through it with a pair of powerful shears!

"Joe! Stop!"

Joe instantly braked. Even before the car screeched to a halt alongside the kerb, Frank had opened his door. He jumped out and sped towards the crouching figure. Joe swiftly followed.

"Guards!" Frank shouted.

Startled, the broad-nosed, stockily built man whirled to his feet, then glanced quickly back at the alerted guards. The next instant he hurled the shears directly at Frank.

"Look out!" Joe yelled, in horror.

His brother ducked as the lethal blades spun crazily past, missing his head by inches! Frank and Joe sprinted in pursuit of the fleeing man. A guard's voice rang out.

"Stop him!"

But the fugitive was darting across the street, heedless of the heavy traffic. When the boys reached the other side, Joe spotted their quarry leaping into a black saloon a block away. It roared off in a cloud of petrol fumes.

"Did you get the number?" Frank panted.

Joe shook his head. "There was another man at the wheel and the motor was running."

Three security guards ran up to the Hardys.

"We certainly owe you boys our thanks," a tall, round-faced officer said, holstering his pistol. "Confidentially, it's internal security that seems to be our problem."

"You mean there's a security leak at Micro-Eye?" Frank asked, as the group walked back towards the main gate.

"We have reason to think so," a burly guard replied, "despite the careful screening and clearance of all plant workers."

Two other guards had already retrieved the wire cutters but admitted they probably had no fingerprints, since the man had worn gloves. At the Micro-Eye guardhouse Frank and Joe gave a detailed description of the escaped man, who had sideburns and a dark complexion.

"He may be foreign-born," Joe remarked.

At this, the round-faced officer glanced at the other guards, then turned to the Hardys. "We already suspect that aliens who entered the country illegally are operating in this area. Your description may be a great help to us."

"You mean—spies?" Frank inquired.

The officer nodded, but did not reveal any more details. He thanked the boys for their vigilance, then the Hardys returned to their car and headed homewards.

"Spies!" Joe exclaimed. "Just our luck to let one get away! He had some nerve, trying to cut through the fence in broad daylight."

Frank grinned. "Maybe we can pick up another clue for Micro-Eye."

A sharp eye for clues came naturally to the brothers. They were sons of Bayport's renowned private detective, Fenton Hardy, formerly of the New York police force. Joe was impetuous by nature, Frank more deliberate. Ever since solving their first mystery, they had helped their father track down criminals and proved their courage and abilities as independent sleuths. Recently they had faced a dangerous challenge in a case known as *The Sinister Signpost*.

"Too bad Dad isn't here," Joe said. "He'd certainly be interested in what happened at Micro-Eye."

"Yes. His new case really must be hush-hush. He didn't even leave an address."

The car turned into the drive of the Hardys' attractive, tree-shaded house at the corner of High and Elm streets. The boys lugged two huge boxes of groceries into the kitchen.

"Whew! I'll be glad when Mother gets back!" Joe exclaimed. "We keep running out of everything."

Mrs Hardy was away visiting relatives, and was expected to be gone for two weeks.

"I wonder how Aunt Gertrude's enjoying Rio," Frank mused. Their peppery maiden aunt, Mr Hardy's sister, had been in South America since earlier in the summer.

"Brazil will never be the same again," Joe quipped, "but I can't wait until she's back. If I have to live through any more of your cooking—"

Frank laughed, and went for the mail. He returned with a stack of envelopes. "Guess we can't forward these to Dad." He held out four letters addressed to their father.

There was also a blue envelope for the boys. When Frank read the enclosed note, his hand flew to his head.

"What's the matter?" Joe asked in alarm.

"It's from Aunt Gertrude! She says she'll arrive in Bayport on the *Dorado* in eight days. This is postmarked eight days ago!"

"Today!" Joe groaned. "And this place looks as if a hurricane had hit it!"

Frank phoned the North Lines office and learned that the *Dorado*, a freighter, was due to dock early that evening. "Joe! The dishes and beds! Where's the furniture polish? If Aunty finds the house in this shape, we'll really get a lecture!"

The whisk of brooms, the whirring of the vacuum, and the clang of pots and pans filled the air as the boys feverishly cleaned the house from attic to basement.

"Well, that should do it." Frank sighed as the exhausted pair sat down to a light supper. But suddenly Joe jumped up.

"The laundry! There must be a mountain of it upstairs in the hall cupboard!"

The boys charged up the stairs and gathered the crumpled garments and linen. While Joe tied it up, Frank checked his father's wardrobe and removed two pair of slacks which needed cleaning. As he did so, Frank noticed some papers bulging from the inside pocket of one of Mr Hardy's jackets.

"Looks as if Dad forgot these," he called. "Hope they weren't important. Say, we've only ten minutes before the cleaner closes!"

"We can go from there to the pier."

Frank drove into town and parked in front of Corporated Laundries' large new shop which handled dry cleaning.

As Joe ran in with the bundle, a burly, middle-aged man pushed ahead of him to the counter.

"I want these shirts done special. Charge it to my account," he announced loudly.

"Yes, sir, Mr North!" said the attendant, a thin, man with bushy eyebrows. But the overbearing customer had already stalked outside. Joe left his bundle, then rejoined Frank.

"Some nerve!" Joe growled. "Orrin North just elbowed me out of the way in there," he told his brother, as they headed towards the Bayport waterfront. "Even if he does own a shipping line, he could use some manners!"

"They say his passenger business isn't doing so well these days," Frank said. Both boys knew North as a prominent Bayport resident who prided himself on being a successful man.

When the Hardys reached the waterfront, Frank parked at the North Lines pier where the *Dorado* would dock. The customs area bustled with officials. At several piers the boys noticed watchful plainclothesmen.

"There must be something to what that Micro-Eye guard said about illegal immigrants," Joe observed.

"A person would have to be pretty clever to get through all these precautions," Frank said. He turned to a customs inspector and learned that the *Dorado* was expected in an hour. The man added that the ship was taking very few passengers these days.

"I guess Aunt Gertrude was lucky," Joe said. "What say we take a spin in the *Sleuth*? We can watch the *Dorado* coming in and still be back here by the time she docks!"

"Good idea!"

In minutes the brothers reached the boathouse where their sleek craft was berthed. Frank started the motor and pulled out into the sunset-golden waters of Barmet Bay.

Darkness was falling by the time they headed down the coast. Soon Frank sighted the big hulk of an approaching vessel, plying lazily through the long swells. Joe grabbed the binoculars.

"She's the *Dorado* all right. Maybe we can spot Aunt Gertrude on board."

Frank circled nearer the lighted ship, and followed a parallel course, hugging the coast. The boys looked in vain for the tall, straight figure of their aunt. Above the deck a ghostly plume of smoke curled up into the night sky.

"She may still be below," Frank began. "If—"

Crack! Crack!

"Joe! Those sounded like pistol shots!"

"From the *Dorado*! Look, there's a commotion at the stern!"

The boys saw several men scuffling at the fantail of the freighter. The next instant a figure leaped over the rail and plunged into the dark waters!

Instinctively Frank sent the *Sleuth* speeding to the rescue. Soon Joe spotted a bobbing form, and a few minutes later pulled a gasping, sputtering man aboard.

Slender and dark-complexioned, with a thin moustache, he was dressed in a crewman's blue uniform. A quick examination showed no wounds, but the stranger seemed too exhausted to speak. The boys made him comfortable and Frank sped past the *Dorado* and back in the direction of Barmet Bay.

Joe shouted above the noise of the engine, "I wonder who he is and what all the excitement was about."

"Beats me. But we'll have to contact authorities on shore pronto," Frank said worriedly. "Let's just hope Aunt Gertrude's all right!"

Instead of going to their own boathouse, he pulled into the end of the public dock. The crewman revived, and the boys helped him out of the *Sleuth*.

Frank said, "I'm Frank Hardy and this is my brother Joe. We don't know what—"

"Hardy—you said—Hardy?" The man, speaking broken English, was plainly startled.

Before he could say more, a stranger strode briskly up to the trio. He was short and bald, and he wore a badge on the lapel of his black raincoat. He grasped the crewman's arm and snapped:

"The *Dorado* radioed us about you. I'm an immigration officer. Come along! You kids can beat it now."

Suddenly the crewman shook loose and his fist rocketed against the stranger's jaw! The officer staggered back with a grunt.

Frank grabbed at the sailor, but the man dodged and ran, turning only for a fraction of a second to hiss, "Footprints will get—"

He raced off the dock on to the road and was swallowed up in the darkness.

· 2 ·

Night Prowler

"AFTER him!" Frank shouted.

He and Joe ran from the dock and down the road in pursuit of the crewman. They heard footsteps pounding rapidly ahead, then Joe saw a shadow dart between two small bay-front buildings.

"There—to the right!"

The Hardys dashed through back yards and a deserted alley. But the man had vanished. Finally Frank and Joe gave up the chase and hastened back to the docks. "We'd better see if that immigration officer is hurt," Frank said.

When they reached the dock, there was no sign of the short man with the badge.

"Maybe he went to alert his office that the man escaped," Joe said.

"If he *was* from the immigration office," Frank cut in. "There was something phoney about his telling us to 'beat it.' "

Joe agreed. "At any rate, we'll report this."

" 'Footprints'!" Frank mused, recalling the crewman's strange words. "What could that mean? And whom are they going to 'get'—us?"

Joe shook his head. "That man seemed to know our

last name! Where did he find out? Did you notice his accent? Sounded like South American Spanish."

The Hardys hurried to the customs office and gave a detailed account of the recent events. The man in charge took down the information. When Frank described the bald man who had claimed to be an immigration officer, the customs man made a quick telephone call. He hung up, puzzled.

"No one like that works for Immigration," he said. "We'll look into this. Thanks, boys."

The Hardys hurried to the pier where the *Dorado* had just docked. Only a handful of passengers debarked from the gangway, but Miss Hardy was not among them. Worried, Frank and Joe spoke with a uniformed customs inspector.

The official consulted a short list of passengers. "We have no such person listed."

Frank and Joe exchanged dumbfounded glances. "Are you sure there's no mistake? We're expecting our aunt," Frank insisted. Just then a heavy-set man wearing a blue cap approached.

"Boys, here's the *Dorado*'s skipper—Captain Burne. You can ask him."

The newcomer seemed to be distressed as he hurried up to the inspector.

"Mr Clark, we have a missing stowaway thief to report!" the captain announced. "We tried to stop him but he jumped overboard, and—"

"We picked him up but he got away again," Joe put in quickly. He and Frank introduced themselves, then related their experience.

The captain stared in surprise at the boys.

"Captain," said Frank, "isn't there a Miss Gertrude Hardy on your ship—from Rio de Janeiro? She's our aunt, and wrote to us that she'd arrive tonight on the *Dorado*."

Burne shook his head. "Nobody by that name aboard. Only nine passengers this trip—the last time we'll take on passengers."

"Maybe your aunt decided to stay longer in Rio," Mr Clark suggested. "Don't worry, boys."

"I guess she must have changed her mind," Joe said, relieved that their aunt had not been exposed to the shooting incident. The Hardys now asked the captain about the escaped stowaway.

"Is he really a thief?" Frank asked.

"You bet he is!" Burne fumed. "Stole a crew uniform, cleaned out a cashbox in my office, then shot at us when we went after him. He must have sneaked aboard in Cayenne." The captain's eyes narrowed. "Did you boys get any leads on where he went?"

"No." Frank signalled Joe with a glance not to mention the stowaway's peculiar warning to them about "footprints."

The captain shrugged. "Well, at least you got descriptions of him and that phoney immigration officer. If you two get any clues, will you inform Mr North's office?"

"We'll keep our eyes open," Frank promised.

Still a bit uneasy about Miss Hardy, the brothers returned the *Sleuth* to their boathouse, then drove home.

"Aunt Gertrude must be having a ball," Joe ventured.

Frank laughed wryly. "All that house cleaning for

nothing! But," he continued, "this stowaway thief puzzles me. Why was he so startled at hearing our name? I think we'd better find out more about it before we mention 'footprints' to anybody."

The boys decided to try getting word to their father by phoning Sam Radley. Sam was an ace detective and assistant to Fenton Hardy.

"I'll do my best to contact him, Frank," Sam promised. "Sounds very strange. Keep me posted."

After a snack of milk and biscuits, the brothers went to bed. A fresh summer breeze came through the window of their upstairs room in the quiet house.

Some time later, Joe awoke from a sound sleep. He squinted groggily at the radium clock. "Two A.M. What—" He stiffened. Was it his imagination or did he hear a noise downstairs?

A muffled, scuffing step was barely audible, then there was silence. Joe sat up and listened. *Clump, clump!* This was followed by the creaking of a floor board!

Joe shot out of bed and roused his brother, who was awake in a flash. They stood poised at the doorway.

Scuff, scuff! Silence again.

"A prowler!" Joe whispered.

"Let's jump him—quiet!"

With fists tightly clenched, both boys inched out into the hallway. Peering into the darkness downstairs, Frank could barely make out a tall figure starting up the stairs! Crouching forward, Frank and Joe waited, tensing their bodies like taut bowstrings.

"Now!"

Instantly the two thundered down the stairs. As

Frank grabbed the shoulders of the intruder, a high scream filled the hallways.

"*Eek!* Stop! Help! Murder! Bandits!"

Utterly astounded, Joe darted to a wall switch. Light flooded the scene, revealing a dishevelled, struggling woman wildly swinging her handbag.

"Stop! Let go of me—my goodness! Frank Hardy!"

"*Aunt Gertrude!*"

Wordless with amazement, the two boys helped Miss Hardy into an easy chair.

"Gee, Aunt Gertrude, we thought you were a prowler!" Joe said sheepishly.

"Are you all right, Aunty?" Frank gulped. "Can we get you anything?"

"Of course I'm all right!" their exasperated aunt puffed, fanning herself with a ribboned straw hat. "Through no thanks to you, Frank and Joe Hardy! A prowler—humph! Fine greeting from my two nephews after all these weeks!"

The boys apologized profusely, and Frank added, "We're sure happy to see you home safe. We've been pretty worried about you."

Joe spoke up. "Aunty, when and how did you get here? We met the *Dorado* tonight but you weren't on it."

"I should have cabled you that I wasn't coming on that run-down old freighter," she explained. "They wouldn't take any more passengers than they had already booked."

Miss Hardy had sailed instead on a North Lines passenger ship, the *Capricorn*, which had docked just before midnight. The ship had been due the following day but had made better time than expected. Her travelling companion, Mrs Berter, had driven her home.

"I tried not to disturb you boys, but look what happened! I thought I was being attacked by Amazon head-hunters!"

"You pack a pretty mean handbag yourself, Aunty." Frank laughed. "Did you have a good time? How was Brazil?"

"Wonderful," replied Miss Hardy. She rose and gave the room an appraising glance, then nodded slightly, as if pleased to see no dust on the furniture.

Joe grinned. "Pretty good housekeepers, aren't we? But we still had time for running into some mysteries."

"Mercy! I should have known!" Aunt Gertrude pretended to disapprove of her nephew's sleuthing, but secretly was proud of their successes.

Frank and Joe described the day's events, concluding with the escaped stowaway. "You missed all the excitement, Aunty, by not sailing on the *Dorado*," Joe added.

"Not exactly," Miss Hardy said in a mysterious tone. "I had an adventure on shipboard myself."

No amount of persuasion would induce her to explain further. "It's far too late. You'll have to wait until I'm rested."

With that, Aunt Gertrude marched upstairs. The boys, bursting with curiosity, picked up her bags and followed.

· 3 ·

Missing Papers

AUNT GERTRUDE had another surprise waiting for her when she entered the kitchen the next morning.

"Breakfast is served!" Joe's voice rang out. She stared in astonishment as her younger nephew turned away from the stove. "Morning, Aunty! Here's bacon. Frank will have your eggs ready in a minute."

"Less than that!" Frank lifted a skillet from the range. He grinned. "Sizzling omelet!"

"Well, you two must be up to something," she said as Joe pulled out her chair and she sat down. "But this *is* thoughtful of you," she conceded. "You must have wakened early!"

Their aunt was customarily the first one up in the morning. Frank stifled a yawn as he served the slightly burned omelet, then winked at his brother.

"Of course this is temporary, isn't it, Joe?"

"You bet. We wouldn't put one of the world's best cooks out of a job—no sir!"

Aunt Gertrude eyed the boys suspiciously as they took their places. The two immediately beseiged her with questions. "Was South America exciting?" Joe began.

"Very. And perilous," she replied. "Full of animals, insects, spies—" She picked a piece of shell out of her omelet and sniffed.

"Aunty," Joe coaxed, "what about this—er—adventure you had on board ship?"

Miss Hardy put down her fork. "Well, first of all," she said, "there were those luggage thieves."

"Luggage thieves?" Joe echoed.

"Yes. I met poor Mr and Mrs Taylor at a stop-over in Cayenne—the capital city of French Guiana. They're from around here—Harpertown, and were travelling by plane. Almost the minute they arrived at the airport, all their bags were stolen. The thieves got away."

The discussion was interrupted by the squeal of brakes outside.

"Chet!" Frank exclaimed. "He's never up this early during vacation!" But a rap on the back door and the appearance of a plump boy with a round, freckled face affirmed the fact that the caller was the Hardys' best friend, Chet Morton.

"Howdy, breakfasters!" he sang out. "Why, Miss Hardy, welcome home!"

"Thank you, Chester." Aunt Gertrude smiled and invited the newcomer to join them.

"What brings you out of the sack so early?" Joe asked him.

Chet explained that he was on an errand for his father at Oak Hollow, where a housing development was nearing completion. Mr Morton, a real estate agent, was handling prospective sales.

"But I sure worked up an appetite on the way," Chet

added, looking hopefully at Miss Hardy. He sniffed the aroma of toast and bacon. "Any crumbs left over?"

"Aunt Gertrude's our guest this morning," Frank informed him, handing over three eggs, "but you're welcome to cook your own grub." In a flash Chet had eggs scrambling in the pan.

Joe asked him, "Say, have you seen any stray stowaways floating around?"

"Wha-at?" Chet stared at his pals. "Oh, no! You're not mixed up in another mystery!"

The stout boy was not fond of danger, but had often become involved with the brothers' cases, and always proved a loyal assistant. While Chet ate, the Hardys brought him up to date.

"I'd like to track down that fellow who jumped overboard," Joe said. "Something tells me he was trying to give us a message."

Miss Hardy, obviously enjoying herself, continued her story. "Even stranger doings on the *Capricorn*, though. A man disappeared."

"Disappeared!"

The boys waited patiently while Miss Hardy paused for a sip of coffee. Then she told of having met a very nice gentleman on the homeward trip, a Mr Ricardo. She had not learned his first name. "He had heard of your father and asked me questions about Fenton's latest case—even wanted to know where he was." Miss Hardy described the man as tall, with an angular face and wearing a white suit and dark glasses.

"He was very pleasant," she continued, "but of course I couldn't answer his questions. Then—all of a sudden—he vanished."

"From the ship?" Joe asked, incredulous.

"Yes. I went to say good-bye to him a few hours before we docked and he was gone!"

"Maybe he was ill," Frank suggested. "Did you try the ship's infirmary?"

"Yes—not a sign of him. And the stewards weren't very helpful. I'll never travel North Lines again," she added. "I only hope nothing awful happened to the poor man."

"Sounds weird to me," Frank mused, recalling the *Dorado* stowaway's familiarity with the name Hardy. Was there any connection?

Their aunt stood up. "Before you start sleuthing, I have some work for you to do."

"But, Aunty," Joe protested, "we've already cleaned the house!"

"We'll see about that."

Chet chuckled as the brothers shrugged helplessly. After the dishes were rinsed and put in the washer, Chet grabbed an apple and the trio trailed Miss Hardy through the downstairs rooms. Armed with a dustcloth, she probed with eagle eyes into every corner and under the cushions of the living-room furniture.

"Well," she conceded, "maybe you did touch the high spots—*tsk*, look at this dust!" She ran a finger along a chair leg and held it up disapprovingly. The boys exchanged grins.

"We even swept out the cupboards," Frank defended himself.

Next, Miss Hardy carefully inspected the upstairs rooms.

A little later Frank opened the cupboard in his

father's room. Suddenly he stared at the jacket which had contained the papers.

The inside pocket was empty!

Frantically the boys checked the entire cupboard, but the papers were not there. Aunt Gertrude said she knew nothing about them.

"Are you sure they were here?" Chet asked.

"Positive!" Frank said. "Joe and I both noticed them yesterday. *Somebody else has been in this house!*"

Immediately a thorough search was begun. Finding no clues to the intruder, the boys went outside.

"Whoever he was, he's a pretty slick operator," Joe said, "but he may have dropped something in our grounds."

While he looked round the garage, Frank and Chet inspected the area near the house. Suddenly Frank yelled, "I've found something!"

The others rushed to where he was kneeling beneath a window. Frank pointed to the ground.

Several impressions were visible in the soil directly beneath the sill of the dining-room window.

"Footprints!"

"Just the front part of the soles," Frank observed. "These marks look fresh, and neither Joe nor I was out here recently. The prowler had an easy time getting in since the window's unlocked."

Joe ran up to their lab over the garage and returned with a fingerprint and cast kit. Together, the three boys checked the window sill and the dining-room, but the thief appeared to have left no clues.

"He must have been wearing gloves," Frank said, recalling the man they had chased at the Micro-Eye plant. In the next instant another thought struck him. "Joe! The *Dorado* escapee!"

"Jimminy, I forgot all about him!"

"What do you mean?" Chet asked, puzzled.

Frank repeated the cryptic reference to "footprints."

"You think he's the one who stole your dad's papers?" Chet asked.

"It's just a guess," Joe replied. "He's been accused of stealing money on the freighter, and besides, he did seem to know our name."

"But why would anyone warn us in advance if he meant to break into the house?" Frank argued. "It could have been a warning about somebody else. But it sounds crazy that he could've known what sort of clues that person would leave, when he had just jumped off a ship from Cayenne."

The others watched as Joe took a cast of the shoe tip. The Hardys were dissatisfied. "If only he had left a heel print!" Joe complained.

"It looks like about a size ten shoe," Frank remarked, making a mental note of the distinctive cracks in the sole.

Chet shrugged. "That narrows it down to a few million men. Were your dad's papers important?"

"We don't know," Joe said. "They must have been for somebody to steal them. We'll be lucky if we can get in touch with Dad to tell him."

They took the completed cast to the garage lab, then went to the house. Frank telephoned Sam Radley again, but was disappointed to learn that Radley had been unable to locate Mr Hardy.

After telling the operative about the theft of the papers, Frank asked, "Shall we notify the police?"

"I'll talk to them," the assistant said. "If I hear from your dad, I'll call you."

As Frank reported the conversation to the others, the brothers became apprehensive. Had anything happened to their father?

"Well, I certainly hope not," Aunt Gertrude said. "But don't you worry about any more desperadoes getting into this house! I'll be on guard!"

The boys smiled. "We'll leave that to you," said Joe, "while we pursue the mystery."

Chet sighed. "Look, fellows, I'll help. But first, how about you driving out to Oak Hollow with me?"

"Okay!"

The three boys piled into Chet's jalopy and in minutes were heading towards the outskirts of Bayport. Oak Hollow was a small, shrubbed valley which had lain remote from the town's progress for many years.

The construction of attractive, medium-priced homes there had been undertaken by the father of another friend of the Hardys, Tony Prito. Frank and Joe had not visited the site since the early stage of development, and were interested to see the completed houses.

"When will owners be able to move in?" Joe asked as they wound up a hill road.

"In a week or so," Chet replied. "This development will be great for Bayport, and Dad's real excited about it."

They turned down a muddy road past large construction vehicles and a row of handsome frame houses, each separated by wide, newly seeded lawns.

"Wow!" exclaimed Joe, impressed.

"And they're not all alike," Chet added. "I'll show you a model."

As the jalopy neared the end of the street, the boys were startled to hear a chopping sound, followed by the tinkle of glass!

"That sounded like a windowpane!" Joe cried out. "Hey! Look!"

Astonished, the boys saw two men in dungarees outside one of the houses. They were hacking at the wood with machetes!

"Vandals!" Chet gasped, skidding to a stop.

He and the Hardys jumped out and rushed the men. As Frank tackled one, Joe side-stepped a swinging blow and grabbed the other around the neck. But the thug threw him off. Joe lost his footing in the mud and went down on his back.

Stunned, he looked up to see an ugly face and an extended arm. Sunlight glittered off a raised machete!

·4·

Peril in the Air

AN instant before the man swung the machete down in a vicious chop, Joe rolled aside.

Thwack! The blade crunched resoundingly into the ground.

Joe immediately kicked out at his attacker. The man dodged, but Frank and Chet grabbed him, and Joe scrambled to his feet. The next instant the man's partner, swinging his machete, forced the three boys back.

"Come on. Let's beat it!" he snarled.

The two vandals ran behind the house and disappeared into thick woods covering the slope. The three boys took off in pursuit. But as they emerged from the woods, a motor roared to life from round a bend in the dirt road.

"We're too late!" Frank groaned. He pointed to automobile tyre tracks and a cloud of dust.

Back at the development, the boys found Mr Prito and two other men inspecting the damage. Jagged holes gaped in numerous windows, and splintered slashes had been made in the walls and mouldings of many houses.

"The windows are easily replaceable," Mr Prito said, his face grim, "but repairing the other damage will take time. We'll have to delay occupancy for weeks!"

"What a vicious trick!" Joe stormed, stepping over broken glass and fingering a huge notch in a freshly painted door.

"But why would they do it?" Chet said, equally disconsolate.

"I don't know. The whole thing is senseless," Mr Prito said. "We'll have to put on a watchman."

When Mr Morton and the police arrived, the boys provided descriptions of the hoodlums and pointed out the tyre prints. The motive for the vandalism was a puzzle to everyone.

"I know of no rival contractors who might be bitter at not having landed this job," Mr Morton said. "If this was malicious mischief, it's pretty expensive mischief for us."

On a hunch Frank inspected several footprints left by the thugs, but there was no similarity to the partial ones found under the window at their house. The Hardys had just climbed into Chet's jalopy when a man's smirking face peered in at them.

"The early bird gets the worm, eh? Any clues?"

Oscar Smuff, a plump, would-be detective, was well known to Frank and Joe. Keen on proving his ability to Chief Collig of the Bayport Police Department, he actually succeeded more in muddling cases than in solving them. Although he was meddlesome, the Hardys good-naturedly humoured him.

"Nothing much yet," Joe replied.

Smuff cocked his head knowingly. "Well, I'll take a

look round and try to clear this thing up. Call me if you need advice."

"Oh, sure." Joe stifled a grin.

Chet's motor started with a whine, and the jalopy headed east from Oak Hollow.

Joe spoke up. "Now to get down to business. First, we must trace the guy who took Dad's papers, then look for that stowaway, and—"

Chet broke in. "Okay. You two can hunt crooks. I'm off to study the clouds."

"The clouds!" Joe echoed. "You're kidding!"

"I am not. Listen, clouds are really interesting—and I want to learn more about them."

The Hardys grinned. They were accustomed to their friend's taking up one hobby after another. "But why clouds?" Joe asked.

"For weather forecasting. What else?"

Frank had a suggestion. "Say, Chet, you've given me an idea. Maybe we can go for a plane ride. You could study clouds, while Joe and I look at the Micro-Eye set-up from the air."

"Great!" Joe said eagerly. "Let's see if Jack Wayne can take us."

Jack was a young charter pilot who often flew Mr Hardy on long trips. Chet needed no persuasion and drove west towards the airfield. Presently Joe noticed a shabby green saloon car behind them. Two turns later it was still in sight.

"Chet, double back at the next corner—I think we're being tailed!"

Chet obeyed. "Creeps! I hope it isn't those machete men!" he said nervously.

But when the jalopy rounded the block, there was no sign of the saloon. "Guess I was wrong," Joe apologized. They drove on to the airport.

The boys spotted Jack's blue, silver-winged plane inside its hangar. They met the lean, tanned pilot near the end of the field.

"Be glad to take you fellows up," he said, after greeting them warmly. "You're lucky to catch me between taxi jobs." Jack explained that he had been flying scientists in and out of Bayport.

"For Micro-Eye's secret project?" Frank asked.

"Yes. What's going on over there is really hush-hush. Give me twenty minutes to finish some flight reports. Be right back."

As Jack disappeared into the building, the boys strolled over to the terminal. They noticed an elderly man complaining to an official about a stolen suitcase. The Hardys' keen ears caught the phrase "in Cayenne."

"That's where Aunt Gertrude's friends had all their luggage taken," Frank said.

Minutes later, the four were airborne in Jack's sleek *Skyhappy Sal*. Chet chattered excitedly and pointed out various cloud formations.

"They're cumulus clouds," he said, indicating large fluffy masses extending eastward. "And to the south is the stratus layer. The wispy, curly ones you see way up high are cirrus."

"Sounds like a fruit," Joe teased. "But I must say you talk like a scholar, Chet."

The chubby boy beamed as Jack banked into a smoky, towering bulge of cloud. "Boy, at sunrise it must be like diving into candy floss!"

When the *Sal* emerged into the clear ocean of air again, they spotted the Micro-Eye plant below. The panorama revealed long roofs, multiple fenced-off areas, and numerous moving dark specks—workmen and guards.

"Looks just as secure from up here," Frank remarked. "How about a quick pass above Oak Hollow, Jack?"

"Roger! If we start buzzing Micro-Eye, they'll have me on the carpet—and I don't mean a cloudy one!"

High over the outskirts of Bayport, the boys saw the new houses nestling among the wooded slopes, along which ran a winding dirt road. Jack took the plane lower, and Frank and Joe scanned the surrounding terrain. Except for a private, fenced cemetery in the valley and a few picnic areas, there were only woods.

"Do you have some special interest in the housing development?" Jack asked.

The boys told of the vandals, and the pilot whistled. "I wouldn't buy a house there," he remarked, "until those thugs are caught."

Frank said thoughtfully, "That'll be hard on Chet's father. Do you suppose the men using machetes are from a tropical country?"

"Like somewhere in South America?" Joe guessed. "The guy that spoke had an accent."

Jack was now flying south along the coast. He dropped down and circled a large inlet surrounded by a pine barren. Whitecaps washed against countless black rocks which barely projected from the water.

"Cobblewave Cove—and there's the wreck of the old

Atlantis." Joe recognized the tilted hulk of a freighter which lay in the midst of the rocks.

Cobblewave Cove had been a danger to incoming vessels for years. When the *Atlantis* had foundered on the sharp rocks during a violent gale, the wreck had been left as both a memorial to its crew and a warning to other seamen.

"I'd like to explore that wreck some day," said Chet. "Maybe we'd find treasure aboard."

"What!" Joe said in mock horror. "You don't believe the legend of the *Atlantis*?"

Chet waved a disdainful hand. "You mean about wails of dying mariners inside the hold? I don't believe that ghost stuff."

"Brave words, pal." Joe grinned.

Jack began circling to turn northwards. "I'm due back at the field, fellows." But when the craft banked steeply into a stiff wind, they all felt a sudden lurch. Then another!

"What's wrong?" Joe exclaimed, alarmed.

"Don't know—she's not flying right!" Frantically Jack worked the controls. Despite his efforts, the plane snapped to the left. The boys peered out and gasped with horror.

Shredded pieces of metal were streaming from the outboard section of the left wing. A bend appeared about three feet in from the tip.

The outer section then began to flutter violently in the wind, as if making ready to separate itself from the aeroplane!

· 5 ·

Suspect at Large

"THE wing!" Frank cried out. "It's breaking up!"

Simultaneously the Hardys and Chet were flung against their seat belts. The engine screamed. The plane plunged into a downward spiral. After four turns, the gyrations tightened into a spin.

"We must be losing nearly a fourth of our lift on the left wing!" Jack shouted. "Our aileron is almost useless!"

He cut the engine power, shoved full right rudder, and snapped the stick forward. Recovery was slow, but Jack finally manœuvred the plane back to straight and level.

Looking out, the boys saw the damaged wing section still attached. But jagged ribbons of metal were trailing from its lower surface.

"Will we make the airport?" Joe asked.

Jack stared tensely ahead, then glanced back. "We've already stretched our luck, but if we take it slow, we should make it. Don't move around!"

Carefully he guided the craft back to the outskirts of Bayport. Chet, his face white, crouched next to Joe with his fingers crossed. "M-me and m-my big hobbies!" he groaned.

In silence Jack manœuvred the plane skilfully out over Barmet Bay. Descending, he banked west towards the airport. Minutes later, he brought the craft to a safe landing. Relieved, everyone climbed out.

Jack and the boys looked at the damaged wing. The pilot frowned. "I don't understand how it could've happened."

The outer section of the wing hung slightly awry from an uneven breach in the metal. Aghast, Joe spotted several dents around the cut.

"This was no accident—the wing was slashed!"

Jack grimly affirmed Joe's suspicion of sabotage. "One clean blow—clean enough for us not to notice it before taking off. The wind did the rest. It could have been an axe—"

"Or a machete!" Frank broke in. "That green saloon behind us on the way here—maybe those vandals were tailing us, and did this job."

"For revenge!" Chet said, rolling his eyes in fear.

Frank disagreed. "That's a pretty strong dose of revenge coming from vandals—unless they aren't just vandals."

Jack led them back to the hangar. "Whoever slashed the wing was willing to take me into the nose dive too. I'm wondering if it had any connection with my taxiing scientists who are working for Micro-Eye. I've flown several of them."

"You mean somebody intended to put a cog in the plant's project—to slow it down?" Joe asked.

"It's possible," the pilot said grimly. "I hope he doesn't try again."

At the hangar one of the ground crew informed Jack

and the boys that he had seen two swarthy strangers leaving the field in a run-down green saloon. His descriptions fitted the vandals.

Joe whistled. "You're right, Frank. Those two are mixed up in something worse than house-wrecking."

Frank nodded. "All we have to find out is—what?"

Jack promised to notify them of any leads, then the three sleuths returned to the jalopy and headed back to Bayport.

Chet spoke up glumly. "From now on, I'll study clouds from the ground!"

Frank nudged his brother. "We can always use a weather prognosticator. Right, Joe?"

"You bet. How's the forecast for sleuthing?"

"Stormy! That I can tell you." Hopefully Chet changed the subject. "Say, don't forget about our going to Cobblewave Cove!"

"Okay, we'll make it soon," Joe said.

Chet dropped the brothers off at Elm and High and chugged along homeward. Frank and Joe headed up the walk to their house.

"Maybe there'll be some word from Dad," Frank said. "We've—" He broke off abruptly. A man was peering at them from behind a large spruce tree across the lawn. The Hardys started towards him, but the man ran off.

"He's the stowaway!" Joe cried out. "Stop!" But the slender fugitive leaped a hedge and tore across the street. Joe bounded off the kerb in pursuit, but was grabbed by Frank just as a car swerved to avoid hitting him. By now their quarry had disappeared. After searching the neighbourhood for twenty minutes without luck, the brothers returned home.

"Boy, he's a slippery eel," Joe said, as they went inside.

"I can't figure him out. Was he spying on us, or—"

"Spies!" Aunt Gertrude sailed into the hall. "Who? Where?"

Frank quickly explained. Miss Hardy's lips tightened. "More desperadoes!" she exclaimed. "What is this house coming to?"

Frank and Joe had decided not to mention the machete attack or plane sabotage. Their aunt told them Sam Radley had called. "He still hasn't heard from your father," she added.

Disappointed, the boys followed their aunt to the luncheon table. Joe sighed. "Well, if we wanted a mystery, we sure got one. Do you think that fellow was casing our house?"

"He acted that way. I wonder if he took Dad's papers, and came back to steal some others," Frank speculated. "Could be he's part of a plot against Dad."

"But why? Dad's not even home. But maybe the guy doesn't know that."

Frank's eyes narrowed. "The *Dorado* thief's from South America," he reasoned. "And maybe those vandals are, too."

"I wouldn't bet against it. Sure wish we could consult Dad."

"First thing we'd better do is report to the immigration people," said Frank.

When the meal was over, the brothers drove to the dock area and pulled up at a small building which housed the office of the United States Customs and Immigration departments. The boys were directed into an inner office where a young immigration officer named Scott sat at a desk.

The Hardys introduced themselves and Frank explained their two contacts with the *Dorado*'s escapee.

The officer nodded. "We've been giving your first report close attention. You're sure it was the same man you saw this morning?"

"Yes, sir," Joe replied. "Dark-complexioned, slender, with a thin moustache. But this time he had on old faded clothes."

Scott snatched a sheet of paper and quickly took down the information. Suddenly Joe noticed two well-dressed men standing at a nearby desk, obviously taking an interest in the boys' statements.

The young officer, meanwhile, knit his brows and drummed his pencil. "Very odd," he said. "The switchboard operator reported that a man came here this morning to see me. I was out. Her description of him matched the one you gave of the stowaway last night—except today's caller wore no uniform, and was poorly dressed."

The revelation was perplexing. "It sounds crazy," Frank remarked. "A wanted thief daring to show up at your office. What did he want?"

"Information, apparently. He mentioned several South American names and asked if any such persons from the Huella Islands had ever sought political asylum in this area."

The Huellas, Frank and Joe recalled, were an island group off the coast of French Guiana, South America.

The largest of them, Baredo, had been in the news recently due to the repressive actions of its ruler, Juan Posada, a dictator known to be unfriendly to the United States.

"But we have no record of anyone arriving from the Huellas," the officer added. He showed the list of names to the Hardys, but they recognized none of them.

Mr Scott shook their hands. "We appreciate your help. We're concerned these days with illegal entrants, since some of them may be sent here for espionage purposes. This escaped man could actually be assigned to spy on Huellan refugees, some of whom may be in or near Bayport without our knowledge."

He added that the bald immigration officer the boys had met was an impostor. "The authorities would like to get hold of him too."

"We'll keep a sharp lookout for both men," Frank promised.

The Hardys said good-bye and hurried across the office. "We must find out more about this 'footprints' business," Joe muttered.

As they reached the doorway, the Hardys were astonished to find their path suddenly blocked by one of the two strangers they had noticed.

"Just a minute!" he said. "You boys aren't going anywhere!"

6

Waterfront Sleuthing

THE HARDYS stood dumbfounded as the tall, expressionless stranger rooted himself firmly in the doorway.

"There must be some mistake—" Frank began. A voice from behind cut him off.

"No, there's not, boys. Come with us. We'd like to have a word with you."

They turned to face a distinguished-looking greyhaired man, the other stranger Joe had seen. The boys started to protest, then saw Scott nod reassuringly. Puzzled, the Hardys followed the two men into an unoccupied file room.

As the taller man closed the door, the other held out a leather identification case. "Roy Dykeman, United States Intelligence."

Frank and Joe examined the credentials, then handed them back. Dykeman introduced his companion as Mr Crothers, also of Intelligence.

"I'm sorry to detain you, but something you said to Mr Scott caught our attention." Dykeman looked directly at the Hardys. "What do you two know about 'footprints'?"

"Footprints?" Frank glanced at Joe. "Not much,

sir. We heard the word last night, and then we found something at our house later that made us wonder whether there was a connection."

"Will you give us complete details?" Mr Crothers asked. "It's important."

Frank told the men of their experience with the *Dorado* stowaway, including his mysterious "footprints" warning. "We didn't mention this in our statement. We thought it might have to do with a private case of our father's, Fenton Hardy."

"Fenton Hardy?" Mr Dykeman glanced at Crothers. "Please continue, boys."

Joe related the theft of Mr Hardy's papers.

"We've been trying to put two and two together," Frank explained, "but we haven't been able to contact Dad. The papers must be important, if somebody wanted to steal them!"

Mr Dykeman paced the floor. "You were right not to reveal anything that could be detrimental to your father," he stated.

"Do *you* know where Dad is?" Joe pressed.

"Not exactly," the agent replied. "Let me explain. I am here in Bayport to supervise security for a vitally important project." He paused and smiled. "We owe you two boys a debt of thanks for your alertness yesterday."

"You mean—at Micro-Eye Industries?" Frank exclaimed.

"That's right. I know you both can be trusted to keep this matter confidential. Micro-Eye is in danger of espionage by aliens, internally as well as externally. We are counting heavily on your father's help."

"Then Dad's assignment *is* for Micro-Eye?" Joe asked excitedly.

"Yes—but as a field agent. Even Mr Crothers and I don't know where he is. The plot we are up against appears to be extensive geographically."

"You believe that somehow 'footprints' are involved with this plot?" Frank queried.

The intelligence officer glanced at his associate, who nodded slightly. "I can tell you this much—we are aware of a conspiracy to uncover, and perhaps steal Micro-Eye's secret work. We believe it to be centred in South America, and directed from there, and it operates, we think, under the code name Footprints."

"Footprints!" Joe echoed. "Then the stowaway may be part of this plot! And that phony immigration officer too!"

"We'll have to track them down before we know," Mr Crothers replied. "We've had our men constantly watching incoming ships and planes for people entering the country illegally, but they manage to slip in, nevertheless."

Frank and Joe promised their full co-operation. After giving the boys a card with their secret telephone number, the two agents thanked them for the assistance. Outside the building, the Hardys hurried to their car.

"Well, at least we've found out what Dad's working on," Joe remarked. "Hey! Do you think he's in South America?"

"Could be. I wonder if the Footprints members may have infiltrated Micro-Eye. Question is, where do the stowaway and the immigration impostor fit into the scheme?"

"And the machete men," Joe added.

Frank remembered Scott's mention of the Huella Islands. "I'm wondering if those South American names that the stowaway asked about belong to spies or refugees."

"Either way, he sure took a risk showing up at the immigration office," Joe stated.

"We'd better warn Aunt Gertrude to keep an eye out for suspicious-looking South Americans," Frank suggested.

Joe grinned. "Or vice versa." They reached the car and headed home.

As they turned the corner at a warehouse, Frank's attention was suddenly caught by a tall, white-suited stranger crossing the street.

Frank pulled over to the kerb. "That man matches the description Aunt Gertrude gave of the vanishing Mr Ricardo!"

Joe peered out the window as the stranger stepped on to the sidewalk a few yards ahead. Suddenly the man glanced at them through dark glasses and hurried past the car.

"You're right!" Joe whispered. "Angular face and all! Do you think it's just a coincidence?"

"Maybe, but let's see where he's heading!"

The boys waited a few moments, then stepped out and followed the man. They kept a block's distance. But the stranger looked back again, and pulled his panama hat lower over his hawk-nosed face. His pace quickened.

"Looks as if he's on to us. Let's go!" Frank urged.

The white-suited man suddenly cut sharp right and disappeared down a narrow side street.

"Don't let him get out of sight!" Joe urged.

Pretence abandoned, the boys broke into a run. With Frank at his heels, Joe nimbly dodged two labourers shouldering a long metal pipe and whipped around the corner.

Wham!

Joe had collided full tilt with a man, and he fell backwards on to Frank. Both boys landed in a sitting position on the pavement. They looked in astonishment at the roly-poly figure of the man, who was slowly getting to his feet.

Oscar Smuff!

"Oowwww!" Groaning, the would-be investigator glared at the Hardys. "You! You! You would get in my way!"

Smuff, muttering furiously, snatched up a notebook from the sidewalk. He continued to sputter. "You Hardys! Who else would interfere just when I was on the track of conspirators!"

"Of consp—" The boys stared in dismay past the self-styled detective. Their own pursuit seemed hopeless. The side street was deserted.

"What conspirators?" Frank asked, gritting his teeth to hide his irritation.

"Don't know yet," Smuff raged, "but I'm hot on their trail—or was until you two meddling amateurs bumped into me."

"You sort of got in our way yourself," Joe retorted.

Smuff ignored him. He peered round the corner, then darted off after the workers carrying the pipe.

Despite their annoyance, Frank and Joe were curious and followed.

"What's up?" Joe asked. Smuff gave him a reproving look, then whipped out a pencil. His round face glowed with importance.

"The code of the underworld!" he whispered, and waddled faster. "I'm trying to break it!"

Frank frowned. "The what?"

"You'll see. Stick with me and learn something about detecting!" Smuff motioned them ahead to overhear the labourers' conversation.

"If they don't take the pennant this year," one was saying, "they'll never win it. The league is getting too tough."

"Say," the other replied, "I've got peanut butter and jelly today. What'd you bring?"

"Sardine, and a bacon and tomato."

Smuff, perspiring heavily, frenziedly wrote in his notebook.

"Don't you get it?" he asked the boys. "That's all a secret lingo. 'Pennant' is a munitions plot—and 'league' is the explosive! 'Tough' means it's hard to get!"

Frank bit off a smile. "I see. But how about the peanut butter and jelly?"

"Haven't figured 'em out yet—the 'sardine' means the plot'll take place at sea." He detected Joe's grin and grimaced. "You won't laugh when I crack this case wide open."

The workmen placed the pipe in a truck, then leaned against it and opened paper bags. Smuff edged closer as the men took out thick sandwiches. They now noticed the pudgy fellow peering curiously at them. "Want somethin', Mac?" one of the workers called out. Smuff flushed and backed away. The men shrugged and bit into their sandwiches, resuming their conversation.

Joe clapped Smuff's shoulder. "Good luck on the bacon and tomato! Hope they're not too dangerous."

Smuff stalked off indignantly, and the Hardys returned to their car. Joe roared with laughter. "Wow, talk about wild-goose chases! 'Underworld code'—in sandwiches!"

"Think what Oscar the Sleuth could make of a whole menu!" Frank said, chuckling.

The brothers still chafed over the disruption of their chase.

"If only we could have found out where that man was heading!" said Joe. "And *if* he actually is the Mr Ricardo from Aunt Gertrude's ship."

"He certainly wanted to get away from us," Frank added. "It's possible Ricardo planned to disappear from the ship. And I don't like it that he quizzed Aunt Gertrude about Dad."

The brothers' discussion ended abruptly as they approached their car and Frank said, "Flat tyre!" He pointed to the scraps of rubber near the left-rear wheel. There was a gaping gash in the tyre.

"Somebody did this on purpose!" he exclaimed.

Joe yanked open the front door and gasped with alarm. "Frank, look at this!"

Rolls of gouged-out stuffing covered the entire seat. Driven deeply into the driver's seat was the long blade of a black-handled machete!

As Joe grimly whipped out a handkerchief and

wrapped it round the handle, a piece of paper fluttered from the seat. Pasted on it were bits of newsprint forming the message:

A warning: Mind your own business.

Joe asked angrily, "Are you thinking the same thing I am?"

"If you mean the vandals are responsible—Yes." Frank opened the boot and grabbed a jack. The boys rolled out the spare, changed the tyre, then drove home.

"Ricardo—or whoever that stranger is—saw us park here," Joe pointed out. "Do you think he could have doubled back and done the damage?"

Frank doubted this. "I'm sure the man wasn't carrying a machete." He looked at Joe. "It's possible Ricardo and the vandals are in cahoots, though."

The Hardys reached home and hurried inside. Frank glanced into the living-room and gave a cry of alarm.

Aunt Gertrude lay motionless on the floor!

7

Reward or Bribe?

"Aunt Gertrude!"

The boys rushed to her side. With a slight shriek Miss Hardy jumped to her feet.

"Aunty, what happened?" Frank asked with relief. "Are you all right?" The tall spinster quickly removed a curtain rod stretched between two chairs.

"Of course I'm all right!" she snapped, apparently flustered at the boys' sudden entry. "Just—er—slipped and lost my balance. Knocked the wind out of me for a moment."

"Whew, you gave us a scare!" said Frank.

Aunt Gertrude walked quickly to the hi-fi set, snatched a disc from the turntable and slipped it into an album. Frank peeked at the garish orange-and-purple cover.

" 'Limbo for Hot-spirited Latins!' Wow!"

The boys glanced at the curtain rod in their aunt's hands and grinned widely.

"Aunt Gertrude! You weren't trying to do the Limbo!" Joe exclaimed, referring to the "dance" in which one arched backwards beneath a horizontal bar held lower and lower.

"The what? Nonsense!" Miss Hardy picked up a

dustcloth and began vigorously polishing a table. "Silly voodoo music! I was just playing that record out of curiosity."

Joe and Frank winked at each other as their aunt propped the curtain rod in a corner. "How about a Limbo lesson, Aunty?"

"Never you mind, Joe Hardy," she remarked, and changed the subject. "Why, look at that dirt all over your trousers! Where on earth have you two been?"

The boys told of having seen the man they thought was Mr Ricardo, and of their futile pursuit. Aunt Gertrude was astonished.

"You mean he really didn't disappear?"

"It's possible he just wanted it to seem that way," Frank reasoned.

"You boys have too much imagination," Miss Hardy scolded. "I suppose you think Mr Ricardo is a pirate in disguise or some other kind of villain."

The boys asked if there had been any word from Mr Hardy.

"No. Oh, I almost forgot," she added. "There was a telephone call for you boys."

"Where from?" Frank asked.

"Mr North, the shipping magnate, of all people. He called three times, and was very brusque. I almost told him a thing or two about how inefficiently his ships are run!"

"Did he leave a message?"

Miss Hardy reported that North wanted the brothers to come to his office the next morning at ten o'clock to discuss some "important business." The boys were puzzled.

"Maybe he wants some information about the *Dorado* stowaway," Joe said.

After supper the boys checked the machete for fingerprints. There were none.

"But look at this!" Joe exclaimed. "A Cayenne trademark on the blade! This is from South America! We must report our find to Mr Dykeman!"

Frank took a world atlas from a bookshelf, flipped to the back index, and ran a finger down the list. "The Huella Islands," he said, "are off the coast of Cayenne!"

"The stowaway got aboard there," Joe said. "He could be one of the higher-ups in the gang. Anyhow, we'd better get our car fixed."

The Hardys drove to an auto accessories place, and were told that repairs would be finished by morning.

The next day the brothers picked up their car and drove to the grimy North Lines Building. They were ushered into Orrin North's large, plushly furnished office on the top floor. The bulky magnate was relaxing behind a mahogany desk near a picture window overlooking Barmet Bay.

"Glad you could come. Have a seat." Without getting up, North waved the Hardys towards a small sofa. "Like my office, boys?"

"Very comfortable, Mr North," Frank commented. Both he and Joe were at once struck by the disparity between the lavishness of the office and the run-down exterior of the building. They recalled the reports of North's failing business.

"Like it myself," the shipowner admitted proudly. "And it's all mine—planned by me, earned by me, and preserved by me. Shows what incentive will do. Smart kids like you could do as well—if you play your cards right."

Frank and Joe made no comment. It was rumoured in Bayport that North's rise to wealth had not been entirely honest. Each boy wondered what he was leading up to.

The husky tycoon leaned back in his chair. "I understand you boys ran into that thief who jumped ship from my *Dorado*."

"We did," Joe affirmed.

"That's why I called you in. The hoodlum not only stowed away, but stole a good deal of money. The whole business could give my line a bad name! You two got a good look at him and I'll make it worth your while if you can find him for me. By the way, did the fellow say anything?"

Frank replied cautiously, "Not much. He was too weak to talk."

North seemed satisfied. "Too bad. We might have had more luck if you had gone straight to Captain Burne." His voice showed irritation. "Let me hear first if you get any leads."

"Do you know the stowaway's name—or background?" Joe countered.

The burly magnate shrugged. "Not me. Burne thinks he sneaked on at Cayenne. Personally, I have a feeling he's a spy!"

"It's possible," Frank agreed, a bit startled. Had North a motive in saying this? Or was it merely an offhand remark?

North escorted the brothers to the door, where Frank reservedly said they would "keep in touch."

"I guess you boys know the ropes, being sons of Fenton Hardy." He smiled. "What's your dad up to these days? Haven't seen him around. Big case?"

"He's always busy," Frank answered.

Mr North nodded. "Well, boys, don't forget about that reward! By the way, I'd like to keep this thing out of the newspaper."

As the boys walked back to the car, they mulled over the meeting. "Something about Orrin North rings false," Frank concluded. "He doesn't seem to want the authorities to get to that stowaway before he does. Why?"

"Good question," Joe answered. "I'll bet the stowaway stole something besides money, or maybe he's got something on North!"

"Like what?"

"North himself might be part of the Footprints plot Mr Dykeman told us about."

Frank looked doubtful. "He may be involved in some shady financial dealings, but North's too prominent to risk being in a spy racket."

"Guess so," said Joe. "Did you notice how he tried to fish something out of us about Dad?"

"I sure did! Come on. We have some checking to do."

The Hardys drove to the freighter pier. Here they learned that the *Dorado* was on its way back to Cayenne and other South American ports. At the passenger office they found that the name Ricardo was not on the *Capricorn*'s manifest, nor on that of any other ship arriving recently.

The boys returned to their car. "He must have registered under another name," Joe said.

Frank slipped behind the wheel. "We've *got* to find

that stowaway! He's the key to this whole thing."

"Fine, but we haven't any kind of lead." Joe hopped in beside his brother.

Frank snapped his fingers. "Our boathouse! He learned about our owning the *Sleuth* and might have gone there to hide out—or to snoop!"

"Roger!"

Frank followed the road which wound round the bay to the dock area. Suddenly the boys noticed three men in black raincoats stealthily approaching a run-down boathouse. As Frank and Joe watched, two of the men disappeared round the far side of the building. When the third moved along the near wall, they recognized the short, bald man!

"That phony immigration officer!" Frank jolted the car to a halt. "It looks as if they're after someone!"

The impostor by now had scurried inside. At once the Hardys jumped out. Frank signalled Joe to head left. He went to the right of the boathouse. Cautiously they stole through the high weeds surrounding the building.

A harsh voice was audible from within. "You won't get away this time, Gomez! We'll teach you to run out on us!"

Joe was the first to reach the waterside of the boathouse. He inched along the narrow walkway and peered cautiously inside the entrance.

Three men, spread out on the catwalk, were facing a solitary, slender figure crouching on the rear platform. One of his opponents slowly pulled a rope from his pocket. Together, the men converged on the cornered man.

The Dorado *stowaway!*

8

Cobblewave Cove

THE men's steps echoed eerily in the shadowy boat-house as they advanced on the stowaway. Joe glanced over at Frank, who had posted himself at the other side of the entrance.

The fat, bald man paused and rasped out, "Don't give us trouble. Valdez, Walton and I are going to take real good care of you!"

The speaker's two companions—one stocky, the other huge and bushy-haired—kept stalking their prey. The stowaway braced himself defensively. Frank nodded to Joe and shouted, "Hey!"

Startled, the attacking men whirled. "Greber! It's those Hardy kids! Get 'em!" snarled the stocky thug. The boys recognized him at once as the swarthy-faced Micro-Eye trespasser!

His bushy-haired partner lunged at Joe. The youth dodged nimbly and tripped the man, who fell sprawl-ing on to the rickety dock. But he grabbed Joe's leg and pulled the boy down. The two grappled, rolling peril-ously close to the water.

Frank, meanwhile, had charged inside the boathouse. He landed a blow in the midriff of the stocky man, who staggered, half-stunned. A second later the stowaway raced outside!

"Wait!" Frank's cry was choked off by a rope whipped around his throat from behind. Gasping, he tried to get his fingers inside the rope, but it was drawn tighter!

Desperate, Frank jabbed his elbow full force into his assailant's stomach. Taken off balance, the pudgy man teetered, let go the rope, and landed in the water with a splash.

But the next instant something heavy crashed down on Frank's head. He sank to the floor, unconscious.

The young sleuth had no idea how much time passed before he revived and saw Joe's worried face looking down. "Frank, are you all right?"

"Guess so, except my head hurts." Frank stood up and touched a swelling bruise.

"No wonder! You got conked with this." Joe picked up a brick.

"Oh great!" Frank grimaced. "Hey—the stowaway and those other men—where are they?"

"Gone," Joe said glumly. "All three lit off after Gomez. I started to chase them, until I realized you weren't following me."

The Hardys hurried outside. There was no sign of Gomez or his pursuers.

Frank said, "At least we know there's some link between Gomez and the wire-cutter fellow. He must be the one called Valdez—and the big guy is Walton. The other's Greber."

"But why the attack on Gomez by the others?" Frank asked.

"My guess is he cut out from the gang and wants to blow the whistle on his pals. That could explain his stowing away and jumping ship. Also his warning about Footprints."

"But why would he have stolen Dad's papers?"

"Maybe somebody else did."

"Another puzzler. If Gomez does want help, why run away from us?"

The brothers returned to the car and Joe took the wheel. "Better get you home to take care of that bump," he advised his brother.

"Okay. But we'll make some reports on the way. What do we tell Mr North?"

"Just let him know we saw the stowaway. Maybe we can get some information out of him."

A few minutes later they stopped at a drugstore and hurried inside to the two phone booths. Joe dialled the secret number of Mr Dykeman, and told him of their experience at the old boathouse. The agent was doubly alarmed when Joe mentioned the earlier machete warning.

"At least we know the four men are in the vicinity," said Dykeman. "We'll redouble our efforts to track them down."

Frank, meanwhile, had phoned Orrin North.

"Humph!" the magnate sounded displeased at the boy's report. "Too bad you didn't get Gomez—can't pay you for no results."

"Joe and I aren't worried about the money," Frank said coolly. "We'd like to find out what's at the bottom of all this." Hoping to draw the man out, he described the trio pursuing the runaway. "Do you know any of them?"

"Of course not!" North snapped. "If you get something new on that thief, post me at once."

Frank hung up thoughtfully. *Did* North have another reason for wanting the stowaway captured other than the thefts from the *Dorado*?

Back at the house, the boys told Aunt Gertrude a mild version of how Frank had received his bump. She looked worried, however, and insisted Frank apply a cold compress to his head.

Just after lunch they heard the loud squawk of a horn outside. A moment later Chet bounced jauntily into the house. "All aboard for Cobblewave Cove—in the *Sleuth*, I hope!"

"Not today," Joe protested. "We have a few spies to catch up with."

Chet was crestfallen. "Oh, come on, fellows. You prom—" He stopped and stared at Frank. "Wow, what collided with you?"

"A large brick and a few thugs."

Chet's eyes bulged as the brothers brought him up to date. "Whew! Sounds like a fistful of ugly customers! Say," he added coaxingly, "some fresh salt air is just what you need!"

"Well, all right," Frank agreed finally. "We'll take a run out to Cobblewave Cove."

Joe grinned. "What's the weather outlook from the Morton Cloud Bureau?"

Chet held his palm upwards and eyed the ceiling intently. "Excellent! All clear!"

Aunt Gertrude cautioned the boys, "Now don't take chances climbing around that old shipwreck. It's dangerous."

Chet drove the boys in his jalopy to the Hardy boat-house. They were greeted by dark-haired, good-looking Tony Prito. He hurried over from where his motor-boat, the *Napoli*, was moored.

"Hi, mates! You missed the excitement!"

"What? Where?"

Tony explained that police and plainclothesmen had been combing a deserted boathouse up the road. "Must have been some kind of trouble there," Tony said.

"We can vouch for that," Frank said ruefully.

Tony whistled at the Hardys' account of their strug-gle. "Spy suspects!"

The Hardys asked him if there had been any more vandalism at the Oak Hollow housing development. "No," Tony replied, heaving a sigh. "But Dad is sick about it. Making repairs is costly."

He looked sombre upon hearing of the suspected machete sabotage on Jack Wayne's plane. "What does your dad think?"

Frank explained that his father was working in-communicado for the present.

"So you and Joe are prime targets, apparently," Tony said.

"Looks that way." Joe scowled. "Those thugs must be hiding out around Bayport."

Chet impatiently urged that the boys start for the cove, and Tony gladly accepted an invitation to join his pals aboard the *Sleuth*.

Twenty minutes later the sleek craft, with Frank as helmsman, was streaking into a brisk wind down the coast. Its bobbing bow cut blue waves into jewels of salt spray and left behind a foamy, meandering wake.

While Frank, Joe, and Tony discussed the mysteries, Chet stretched out in the stern. "A perfect cumulus!" he announced, pointing to a white fluffy cloud as he munched a chocolate bar. "Yes, it's fair weather ahead, my friends."

Frank throttled down for the turn into Cobblewave Cove. "Too bad Iola and Callie didn't come along." Iola, Chet's sister, was Joe's favourite date, while pretty Callie Shaw was Frank's.

Chet sat up and grinned. "You two detectives have competition—sea shells."

"What?" Joe pretended indignation.

"The girls wanted to go combing for some old shells. Besides, they're scared of the spooky legend about the shipwreck."

By now the *Sleuth* had entered the cove, and was approaching the hull of the foundered ship.

"You don't mean Iola and Callie are really scared by that ghost business," Joe said.

Chet gestured dramatically. "Listen! Just yesterday Iola said she heard reports of horrible cries from deep inside!"

"I thought you didn't believe that hogwash, Chet," Joe said, chuckling.

"Of course I don't!" Chet retorted, but he shifted uncomfortably.

"Ship ahoy!" Frank sang out.

He guided the *Sleuth* past glistening black rocks, banking round the bulky, weather-torn stern of the half-sunken freighter. Beneath thick rust the name *Atlantis* was faintly visible.

The barnacled hull leaned to the north, shored up by a small sand bar beneath the gashed-in port bow. The foreship hung against a toothlike rock formation. Above, two toppled booms ángled over a crushed deck rail. The wreck lay some hundred yards out from shore.

"Old man North must have had a fit when this crate cracked up," Tony remarked.

The Hardys were surprised. "The *Atlantis* was a North Lines ship?" Frank asked.

Tony nodded. "My dad was talking about it the other day. He said the wreck happened shortly after Mr North started in business."

Frank cut the engine as they inched between the rocks near the bow of the ship.

"Let's see if we can board her and have a look around," Joe said eagerly.

He and Tony clambered forward. Tony was first to spot a rusted ladder against the freighter's prow. "We can go up there!"

But Joe had seen something else. "Oh—oh!" He pointed to a warning sign which hung from the bow anchor:

DANGER—DO NOT BOARD THIS VESSEL
TRESPASSERS   WILL   BE   PROSECUTED
ORDER OF U.S. COAST GUARD

"Guess that's official," Frank observed, nudging the *Sleuth* near the ladder. The rung crumbled into flakes.

"It's pretty dangerous all right," he admitted. The boys were disappointed.

Chet shrugged. "There probably isn't any valuable cargo. We'd better go back."

The other boys exchanged winks. "Let the ghosts have the treasure, eh?" Tony needled.

Chet opened his mouth to retort. But instead his eyes widened in fear. "Listen!" Chet squeaked. "I—I heard a scream."

The four listened intently. But the only sound was the gentle lap of the waves. Chet sank back. "Guess it was only my imagination."

The Hardys and Tony laughed as Frank guided the *Sleuth* towards the cove entrance. A white yacht, churning northwards, arced slowly to turn in. Frank steered out of its path. Suddenly the boys noticed the yacht swing about, and at increased speed head directly towards them!

"The skipper must think this is a drag strip!" Frank said, and honked the *Sleuth*'s horn. Still the powerful boat bore down on them.

"What does he think he's doing!" Joe cried out.

Frank signalled again, steering closer to the rocky shore of the cove mouth to make way for the yacht. But still it churned relentlessly towards them, the sleek jaw of its prow slicing out wings of froth. Forty yards! Twenty!

Frank frantically swerved the *Sleuth* to the left, past jagged rocks. Joe, Chet, and Tony waved desperately to the heedless pilot.

Then with horror Tony saw a swirling, shadow eddy dead ahead of their bow. A massive ledge of rock! "Frank! Look out!"

But the waves kicked up by the onrushing yacht rolled against the *Sleuth*, driving it straight for the submerged rock!

·9·

Thief in the Crowd

"THE rock!" Joe shouted. "We're going to hit!"

Grimly Frank swung the wheel hard right, and the *Sleuth* missed the deadly rock by inches. The yacht curved away at the last minute. Now it approached the *Sleuth* at slackened speed.

The craft was handsomely trimmed in brass and about forty feet in length. The boys saw the name of the ship in red letters: *Northerly*.

"Orrin North's yacht!" Joe shouted.

A man in blue uniform stepped out on the bridge as the craft drew parallel with the *Sleuth*.

Frank cupped his hands. "What were you trying to do—run us into the rocks?"

"No, I was trying to warn you about them."

"Warn us!" Frank yelled angrily.

"Yes. Sorry if I shook you up. You ought to keep away from that old wreck. This isn't a safe place to go boating."

"With you around it isn't!" Chet piped up.

There was no response from the *Northerly*. Instead, it swept round in a wide circle and ploughed out of the cove southwards. Frank revved up the engine and steered the *Sleuth* into the open sea.

"Whew!" Chet breathed out. "I could just feel us scraping Davy Jones's locker. You sure did some smart piloting, Frank."

Joe burst out, "Does Mr North think he owns the whole ocean?"

Tony's eyes widened. "Maybe his crew has orders to keep anyone from getting hurt near the *Atlantis*."

"To keep him from getting sued you mean," Joe said, still fuming. " 'Warn us'! I'd like to go back and 'warn' him!"

"I didn't notice North on deck," Chet observed.

Tony nodded. "But I've seen him at the helm sometimes, ploughing round Barmet Bay as if he were a fleet commander!"

The Hardys were preplexed. Why had the *Northerly*'s helmsman risked a collision in order to "warn" the boys? Why not signal?

"There's sure something fishy about North." Joe scowled. "Especially his asking us to find that stowaway."

Frank had steered the *Sleuth* into the mouth of Barmet Bay and cut speed. Now he said thoughtfully, "I have a hunch we should scout around Cobblewave Cove again."

Chet perked up. "Iola and Callie want to do some shell hunting near there tomorrow, at Barren Sands. Why don't you fellows come along?"

"It's a date," Frank agreed.

Tony said he could not join his friends because he would be helping his father at Oak Hollow.

"Call us if there's any more trouble," Frank urged.

"Will do!"

The *Sleuth* was soon docked, and Chet drove the Hardys home. "See you tomorrow." The boy waved and the jalopy chugged away.

Later, Frank phoned Jack Wayne at the airport. The pilot reported he had been in touch with Micro-Eye Industries about the plane sabotage. No clue to the culprits had yet been found, but his plane had been repaired satisfactorily. "And just in time. I'm due to fly to South America in about two days to investigate luggage thefts in Cayenne!"

"Cayenne!" Frank echoed.

"That's right. The airline people here are concerned about the pilfering of baggage there. I know some French, was available, and—thanks to my detective training working with you Hardys—the investigators here think I can handle it."

"Need any help?" Frank asked hopefully.

Jack laughed. "As a matter of fact, I have some extra space. Would you and Joe like to come along? Chet Morton, too."

"Count us in!"

Frank at once spoke to Aunt Gertrude, who gave her consent for the trip. Next, Joe called Mr Dykeman, then Chet, whose response was excited, although apprehensive.

"Don't we have enough danger around here?" he argued. But in a few minutes their friend reported he had obtained permission to go.

"Swell. Lucky we all have up-to-date health certificates and passports."

"Passports to trouble!" Chet prophesied.

During supper the brothers elatedly discussed the

prospective trip. Aunt Gertrude said with a sigh, "I don't know what your father will say about your flying recklessly into the wilds."

Joe grinned. "Dad wouldn't stand in the way of our solving a mystery. Besides, Aunty, *you* were in Cayenne, and got home okay."

Aunt Gertrude looked at her nephews. "Never mind. *I* wasn't trailing thieves—or spies."

The boys feigned surprise. "What makes you think *we* are?" Frank asked.

"Humph. The trouble at Micro-Eye—the stowaway from South America—that man you think is Mr Ricardo—" Her nephews laughed.

After supper the boys tried to fathom what the Micro-Eye project could be.

"It must be a camera of some kind—a real powerful one," Joe surmised, "or else a telescope."

"Whatever it is, I wish we knew," Frank said. "Everything we've run into points to this Footprints spy plot. Yet we don't even know *what* it is they're after!"

Later the boys drove round the waterfront, hoping for a glimpse of the escapee, Gomez. But there was no sign of him. They returned home at ten o'clock and went to bed.

The next morning Frank and Joe drove to the Morton farm to meet Chet and the girls for their shell-hunting date. As the Hardys pulled up the broad drive, Chet and pretty, blonde Callie Shaw came to meet them.

"Hi!" Callie smiled, her eyes sparkling. "I hear you boys are off to South America!"

Joe looked around. "Where's Iola?" he asked.

Chet said his sister had driven into town earlier with Mr Morton to do some errands. "We'll meet her at the dry cleaner's."

The Hardys noticed that Chet seemed downcast. "What's up?" Joe asked him.

"Trouble at the agency," Chet explained. He referred to the Voyager Travel Bureau of which Mr Morton was part owner. The office had been broken into during the night but nothing had been stolen. "It's happened to other agencies, too," Chet added.

"Sounds queer," Joe noted, intrigued. "Wonder what the intruder was after."

"That's what we'd like to know," said Chet as the four young people piled into the Hardys' convertible.

"Try not to worry," Callie told Chet. "Just think of the luscious picnic your mother and I packed."

The plump boy brightened and everyone laughed. Later, Frank parked not far from the Corporated Laundries store. Joe spotted Iola hurrying up the street and went to meet the attractive, dark-haired girl. She carried a large shopping bag filled to capacity.

"Hi, Iola! Here—I'll take that."

"Thanks, Joe. It weighs a ton."

They headed back to the car. Chet's brown-eyed sister chatted excitedly about the sea shells she and Callie had already collected.

"You'll probably find lots more at—Hey!" Joe suddenly felt a jolt from behind. The shopping bag was snatched from his grasp!

Joe whipped around. A stocky man in a black raincoat was running down the street, the bag clutched in one hand. Iola screamed.

"Stop, thief!" Joe yelled, and instantly took off after the fleeing figure, who darted in and out of the throng of pedestrians, and sprinted over a crowded crosswalk.

Leaping ahead, Joe just made the yellow light. The fugitive had spun round the corner on to State Street. Dodging waves of shoppers, Joe ran full steam along the kerb, skirted two parked cars, then made the turn. People kept surging into his way, but he squeezed through the startled crowd and broke into the open. By now the thief was out of sight.

Joe stopped. The bag snatcher could have taken any direction. Disgusted, Joe ran back to Iola. The others were grouped around her.

"Did you get a good look at him?" Frank asked his brother quickly.

"Not his face. From his build, he could be the fellow we chased at Micro-Eye."

With a nervous look round, Chet muttered, "No matter where we go, those spies turn up."

At this, the girls were visibly upset. "Spies!" Iola gasped.

The Hardys explained as much as they felt was politic. Then Frank asked, "Iola, what did you have in the bag?"

"A box of clothes from Corporated Laundries— mostly Chet's, some things for Mother, and a magnifying glass," she murmured nervously. "I think that's all."

"Too bad to lose them," said Joe. "But why would anyone else want them?"

Two policemen arrived on the scene and were given an account by Joe and Iola. The officers, whom the

Hardys knew, were especially interested to learn that Joe thought he recognized the thief. "Let us know if you spot him again. We've been working on that boathouse investigation," one policeman said.

Callie put a comforting arm around Iola and the group returned to the car.

Chet groaned. "He would have to filch *my* duds."

"And *our* magnifying glass," Iola added, managing a smile. "Callie and I were going to use it to study sea shells. Joe, we'll have to depend on your eagle eyes instead!"

Joe called Mr Dykeman. Chet telephoned home. His mother was disturbed by the incident, but she insisted the group did not cancel their plans.

Soon they were driving south towards Barren Sands. They talked of the theft.

"Why should he pick on me?" Iola complained. "Did he figure I had a treasure in the bag?"

"Maybe he took the bag because Joe was carrying it," Frank suggested. "He might have hoped to get some clue to what we're doing."

Half an hour later Frank turned off Shore Road and parked in a little-used lane. The boys and girls trekked through high, coarse grass and came out on the wide, deserted beach of Barren Sands. Just south of it they could see the mouth of Cobblewave Cove.

Callie and Iola immediately kicked off their shoes and began prowling through the surf to find interesting shells. The boys, meanwhile, walked farther down the beach towards the cove. A brisk wind had come up lashing the breakers. Thunder clouds reared up on the horizon.

"Oh, oh," said Chet. "Storm's brewing. But it'll blow over."

Presently Callie called, "Boys, help us search!"

"Let's eat first," Chet insisted.

After a hearty lunch the teen-agers spread out, meeting occasionally to inspect one another's discoveries—ark shells, clam shells, channeled whelks, snail shells, and many more varieties.

"This is probably a New England Nassa." Iola excitedly held up a yellowish spiralled shell.

Joe grinned. "You sound like a professor."

"Look at this one, everybody!" Callie waved from the top of a slope that led down to the water. The others ran up and admired an unusual, conelike shell she had plucked from the sand.

"That's a honey!" Chet said. "What kind is it?"

Callie studied the whitish univalve, about two inches wide with a keyhole groove in its blue interior. Neither girl could identify it.

Just then Frank looked down and noticed something that aroused his curiosity. A circular pattern of large, barefoot prints surrounded the spot where the shell had lain. Before he could comment, someone ran up behind them. They turned to face a swarthy stranger, unshaven and wearing patched clothing and sandals.

He cried out angrily, "Give me that shell! It's mine!"

To everyone's astonishment, he snatched the shell from Callie's grasp!

· 10 ·

Discreet Intruder

"IT's my shell—I found it!" Callie protested. But at the unkempt stranger's savage expression, she stepped back in fright.

"She did find it," Joe asserted firmly. "What's the big idea, mister?"

The man's eyes gleamed suspiciously at the teenagers. Gripping the shell tightly, he started down the slope.

Frank blocked his path.

"Just a minute," he said evenly. "What right do *you* have to this shell? Who are you?"

"I'm called Sandy," the man said sullenly. He jammed the object into his pocket. "I found this shell earlier and put it here."

"That's not likely," Frank disagreed, pointing towards the incline. "Those footprints up there are too big to be yours. Besides, why would you have left the shell here?"

As the others stepped closer, the man shifted uneasily, as if groping for an excuse.

"Please," Iola spoke up, "my friend Callie and I collect shells. There are lots of other pretty ones left on the beach."

73

Sandy shook his head stiffly. "No. I must take this to Mr—" He broke off, then continued, "You see, I sell shells to get enough money so I can eat. It's my only job."

So sudden was his change of manner that Callie relented. "All right, you may keep the shell."

She had scarcely finished speaking when the man marched quickly away. He soon disappeared round a bend in the beach.

"You shouldn't have given it to him, Cal!" Chet insisted. "He as much as admitted he was lying!"

Callie sighed. "Well, he's evidently very poor, and needs the shell more than I do. Maybe we can find another!"

Both Frank and Joe were studying the circle of footprints. "They're damp," Frank observed. "What strikes me is the perfect pattern, as if to mark where that shell was."

Joe then noticed a jumbled series of prints leading towards the water. The brothers followed the trail down the slope. Here they diverged into two distinct sets of tracks—one coming and one going. Both ended at the water's edge.

"Let's separate and see if there are more prints along the beach," Frank suggested.

The Hardys combed the surf in opposite directions. When they rejoined the others later, neither boy had spotted any further trace of footprints.

"Whoever made the prints must have either swum a long distance," Joe said, "or come ashore from a boat."

Chet glanced at the Hardys. "I'll bet you two have *some* theory cooking," he said.

Frank nodded. "That beachcomber's fishy story, these footprints—I'll bet something important was inside that shell."

"A message?" Callie asked.

"It's a good guess," Frank replied.

Secretly he and Joe were wondering if the mysterious prints and shell had a connection with the Footprints plot! "Wild hunch," Frank told himself. "But I'd like to know who's buying that shell."

For the next hour the young people hunted shells, but found none like the beachcomber had taken. Frank and Joe scanned the area in vain for any further sign of the stranger.

Suddenly Chet shouted, beckoning to the others. "Storm's coming up fast!"

The sky was rapidly filling with black clouds. Rumbles of thunder could be heard. Iola gathered the collection of shells into a large kerchief. By this time drops of rain had become a downpour.

The girls and boys dashed to the car and clambered in. Torrents of rain drummed on the steaming roof as they rode home. Joe reminded Chet of his optimistic weather forecast.

Chet, sitting behind with Joe and Iola, asked innocently, "So what am I, a barometer?"

After dropping Chet and the girls off, the Hardys stopped at the immigration office to inquire about Gomez. No trace of him or of the three thugs had been found.

"We've been turning this town upside down," Scott told them. "If the gang hasn't left Bayport, it has certainly found good hideouts."

Back home, the Hardys determined to return to Barren Sands and watch for another possible "pickup" by the beachcomber.

After supper an urgent phone call came from Mr Morton. Chet's father asked the brothers to hurry to the Voyager Travel Bureau. Frank and Joe lost no time in driving downtown.

Mr Morton quickly let them into the street-level office. He looked worried.

"Frank and Joe! Glad to see you! Somebody has broken in here again!"

"When did you find out?" Frank asked.

"Just before I called you. We'd closed up, but I came back for some papers. I was just in time to spot a stocky, flat-nosed man dropping out the back window. I couldn't catch him."

Joe whistled at the description. "Frank! Sounds like the fellow we chased at Micro-Eye—and tangled with in the boathouse!"

Frank asked what had been taken. Mr Morton led them into the back office, switched on a light, and looked around, perplexed.

"That's just it—nothing. Same as before." The police, he added, had found no fingerprints.

"Was *any*thing disturbed tonight?" Frank asked.

"Yes." Mr Morton pointed to a thin sheaf of papers on top of a desk. "Records of our travel customers this week. I found the papers flipped over when I returned from chasing the intruder."

Frank sat down and studied the booking list. It included destinations, tour plans, prices, and means of travel. Most of the clients were Bayport residents.

"What use could these be to an outsider?" Joe wondered, peering over his brother's shoulder.

Mr Morton sank wearily into a chair. "I can't imagine. That's why I called you boys."

Frank continued reading the list. Suddenly he pointed to an entry near the bottom:

Mr Raymond Martin. Cayenne. Jetliner.

"Hmm." Joe's eyes narrowed. "It's the only South American destination listed for tonight!"

"Do you think this is significant?" Mr Morton asked quickly.

"Possibly," Frank replied. He asked Chet's father about Mr Martin.

"I don't know him personally. I believe the arrangements were made by phone." Mr Morton sighed. "The Oak Hollow trouble and now this!"

"It's a puzzle," Frank agreed. "I have an idea, but I'm going to let it simmer until we do some legwork." He asked Mr Morton to notify Micro-Eye Industries of the prowler he had seen.

"Sure will. Thanks for your help, boys."

Outside, Joe started to ask Frank about his idea, but his brother rushed him into the car. "I'll tell you on the way to the airport."

"The airport!"

Frank slipped behind the wheel and headed west. "Raymond Martin," he explained, "is scheduled to leave by plane tonight. We might be in time to get a look at him."

Joe snapped his fingers. "You figure the intruder was after something in particular—like Mr Martin's name?"

"Right—and that could be an alias."

Frank recalled the luggage thefts Jack Wayne was to investigate. "This plane stops over in Cayenne. Martin could either be a possible victim of the thieves —or in league with the spy ring!"

The Hardys parked near the main terminal at Bayport Airport. Inside the spacious building, they quickly found the passenger gate for Flight 54.

"Martin should come through here," Frank whispered, checking his watch. "The plane takes off in ten minutes."

Frank asked the gate attendant if a Mr Martin had yet boarded the plane. The man shook his head. "I doubt it. Nobody by that name has shown me a boarding pass. But he'd better hurry—plane's ready almost for take-off."

The attendant agreed to nod to the Hardys if Martin appeared. Frank and Joe went to stand inconspicuously against a baggage locker nearby and watched boarding passengers file through the gate. Beyond a steel-laced glass wall, landing planes blinked like huge fireflies.

Both boys felt tense. Would they recognize Raymond Martin? Was he an ordinary traveller, or could his name be an alias for Gomez or any of the other elusive suspects?

Five minutes passed. The jets of the silver Brazil-bound liner screamed to life.

"No, you haven't missed him," the attendant assured the Hardys. "Mr Martin's the only passenger not aboard."

"It looks as if he's not going to show up," Joe concluded, disappointed.

"Maybe he spotted us here," Frank said. "Quick! Let's pretend to leave."

The boys hurried off through the crowd. Joe turned his head casually. The next second he grabbed Frank's arm. "Look!"

A middle-aged, well-dressed man was rushing towards the Flight 54 gate, trailing a white raincoat from his arm.

"Wait!" he shouted. "Hold the plane!"

The Hardys were close enough to see that the man's face was completely unfamiliar. As the passenger darted through the gate, his coat hem caught on the end of the metal railing. The man snatched the coat free, but a large piece of lining was torn off and dropped to the floor.

The man did not stop. He ran to the landing ramp and climbed into the jetliner. A minute later the huge craft taxied off and soon rose into the night sky. Frank and Joe stood at the gate staring in chagrin after the plane.

"That was Mr Martin, all right," the attendant affirmed. "Too bad you boys didn't get a chance to speak to him."

Frank retrieved the piece of bright plaid lining, and the brothers walked back across the terminal. "Well, I guess I led us on a wild-goose chase," Frank apologized.

But as he examined the torn material, he noticed a glossy, black edge protruding from a ripped seam.

"Joe, look at this!"

Frank pulled at the edge. A small roll of celluloid fell to the floor!

· 11 ·

A Secret Revealed

FRANK stooped and picked up the celluloid coil from the floor of the air terminal.

"Joe, it's film!"

The Hardy boys examined the torn patch from the stranger's raincoat. A tiny pocket, now ripped, was visible in the plaid lining.

"Pretty clever," Joe murmured. "The film must have been sewn in to avoid detection."

"Something tells me we'd better take a good look at this film," said Frank.

The brothers hastened to a quiet corner of the terminal. Frank unfurled the strip of small film and held it up to the overhead lighting.

"What does it show?" Joe asked excitedly.

"It's hard to make out." Frank squinted up at the tiny frames. "Machinery of some sort—maybe a factory interior—wait! Jumping crickets, look at this!"

Joe grabbed the bottom of the strip and inspected the frame near his brother's thumb. It was an outdoor view showing a high, steel fence and two uniformed figures. Joe gasped.

"The Micro-Eye plant!"

"You bet it is—and taken from *inside* the fence!"

Half-incredulous, the Hardys scrutinized the film's

other frames—close-ups of the complex and labelled diagrams.

"Blueprints!" Joe whispered, as Frank quickly wrapped the spool in the scrap of raincoat.

The boys had no doubt of the importance of what they had come upon: chilling evidence of espionage at Bayport's top-secret project!

"But if Raymond Martin is a spy," Joe wondered, "why didn't he stop to pick up the torn piece?"

"He may not have realized it contained the film. Come on! We're going to get this to Mr Dykeman pronto!"

Frank and Joe surveyed the terminal. Satisfied that nobody had been watching them, they walked to an outside telephone booth where Frank contacted Roy Dykeman.

He urgently related what had happened, but, as a precaution, omitted precise details of the film. The intelligence agent reacted immediately.

"Stay right where you are," he directed tersely.

Minutes later, the Hardys were greeted by two plainclothesmen, who quickly identified themselves with credentials as Miller and Kyle. The boys followed the men out to the parking lot.

Inside the agents' saloon, the boys related what had happened. The men rapidly jotted down notes. When Frank turned over the film, both agents were impressed.

"Great going, boys! Too bad Martin slipped through but he'll be watched when he lands. This evidence could shed light on the Footprints plot. Be careful! We'll be in touch."

The saloon roared off, and the Hardys went to their car. Back home, Joe checked the Bayport telephone directory. A Raymond Martin was listed at a residential address. The brothers took turns dialling the number at intervals, but there was no answer. They found that Mr Hardy's criminal files had no record of the suspect.

The brothers tumbled into bed, but neither fell asleep immediately. Speculations raced through their minds. Who was the mysterious Mr Martin, now airborne to South America?

The next morning after breakfast the Hardys had a phone call from Mr Dykeman. He asked them to come at once to the photographic plant.

Excitedly Frank and Joe dashed outside to their car and in twenty minutes drew up at the Micro-Eye gate. Agent Kyle, to whom they had given the film, looked in at their window, then nodded to the guards.

"Mr Dykeman's expecting these boys," he said.

The Hardys were waved through. They parked in the employees' lot and were escorted by a guard to a second-floor office adjoining the main plant.

Mr Dykeman, looking tired, rose from his desk in the small, map-lined room. His expression was grave as Frank and Joe took seats.

"What you two came upon at the airport last night is a major breakthrough for us," the agent said. "But it's also given us cause for serious concern."

"Then that film was taken by a spy?" Frank asked.

"No question about it. This is proof of an internal security leak at Micro-Eye."

Joe told of the boys' futile efforts to phone Raymond Martin's home.

Dykeman smiled. "It seems he is a highly respected insurance executive who was recently transferred to Bayport. He has no family."

"So he probably isn't knowingly involved in the film business?" Frank queried.

"We believe that's the case," replied Dykeman. "He is going to Cayenne supposedly on business. Of course, Martin *could* be a courier for the espionage ring in Bayport, told to wear the raincoat but not why."

"Which would mean," Joe put in, "that the film was meant to be picked up in Cayenne."

"Yes." Dykeman went on. "We've wired our people there to watch for Martin, and also, for anyone who tries to get his coat. We're hoping the spies won't learn of our recovering the film until after Martin's arrival."

The Hardys were also told that no trace of Gomez or the other three men had as yet been uncovered. The intelligence officer walked to the window and looked across at a long brick building. He turned and smiled at the boys.

"I imagine you're curious about the nature of the Micro-Eye project."

Joe and his brother exchanged glances. "I guess we'd have to admit that!" Frank grinned.

The agent nodded. "We've already had you cleared. You have a right to know the basics of the project, considering your involvement and co-operation in the Footprints case. And because your own lives stand in considerable danger."

Frank and Joe waited tensely.

"In simple terms," Dykeman continued, "Micro-Eye is building a powerful satellite camera."

The boys leaned forward, their interest doubly aroused. "How powerful?" Joe inquired.

"One so strong in range and definition it will be capable of telescoping terrain from the highest altitudes. Even"—he chuckled—"a baby's footprints on a gravel path."

"Wow!" Joe repressed a whistle. "A camera like that would have terrific military value! No wonder spies are after it."

Mr Dykeman explained that after secret project drawings were found missing, the satellite camera's completion had been delayed by "decoy" work undertaken at the plant.

Dykeman held up the familiar spool of film. "Fortunately, whoever took these pictures fell for some phoney blueprints. But we cannot delay the project any more. The government is pressing us."

Frank spoke up thoughtfully. "Since the code name of this spy ring is Footprints, maybe there is a link with the Huella Islands."

"Huella," Joe repeated, then snapped his fingers. "You're right. *Huella* is Spanish for 'footprint'!"

Mr Dykeman and the boys studied a detailed map of South America. Like jagged footprints, the small Huella island group extended north off French Guiana.

"Since the dictator there is unfriendly to the United States, he may well be a party to the plot," Joe suggested.

"Perhaps," Dykeman agreed. "We've discovered that there is great dissatisfaction among the people, even though Posada did away with the infamous prison colony on the island as a concession to them."

"Have you any idea who took the pictures?" Frank asked Mr Dykeman.

The agent motioned the Hardys to accompany him. He led them downstairs and across the yard some distance from the building.

"To answer your question, Frank," he said, in a low tone, "we're turning this place upside down for clues. There are several hundreds of employees, including engineers and technicians. We're running a check on everyone. So far, no suspects. The outside concessions for food and laundry service are kept to restricted areas, and there are constant spot checks at the gate."

"How about the guards?" Joe inquired.

"Thoroughly screened, and all trustworthy," the agent declared. He added that the men's posts were frequently shifted as a double check.

"You think we could have a look around?" Frank asked, glancing over at the main plant.

"I was just about to suggest that." Mr Dykeman fastened visitors' badges to the boys' lapels.

"These will allow you the run of the place," he said, smiling. "Stop back at my office if you come up with any hunches!"

Minutes later, Frank and Joe were touring the interior of the one-storey plant, which hummed with intensive activity throughout its extensive interior. Technicians, intent on their work, scarcely looked up at the boys.

The Hardys were impressed by the steady vigilance of the guards stationed in every department. "How could anybody take unauthorized pictures with them around?" Joe murmured.

"Seems impossible," Frank agreed.

Next, the young sleuths walked through the grounds of the complex. At the isolated maintenance building they were stopped by a heavy-eyebrowed, moustached security guard. He apologized.

"Sorry, boys. Didn't see your badges at first."

After examining the steel fences, the Hardys went back through the main plant.

Joe shook his head. "I can't see a kink in this whole setup," he remarked as they entered the design and draughting section. "This place is as tight as a drum!"

"Sure looks that way," said Frank. "Mr Dykeman has—Joe, look! Up there!"

At the end of the room a security captain and two guards had just seized a slender man in overalls. Draughtsmen gaped in astonishment and the Hardys rushed to the scene. The technician was protesting violently.

Grim-faced, one of the guards snapped, "I just found this in your work jacket, Pryce! You'll have some explaining to do."

He held out a tubular, glass-capped object, then turned to a second guard.

"It's a camera!"

"Stranger" Sighted

"But I know nothing about this camera!" the technician protested. He tried to wrench free from the guards.

The Hardys looked on tensely. Each had the same thought. Had the film they had found come from this odd-looking camera in the employee's jacket? Was he in league with the spies?

The security captain turned the device over in his hands. "Clever disguise. It looks like a tool. All right, Pryce. Come along!"

"Somebody put it into my pocket!" the technician insisted. "This is all a horrible mistake!"

Mr Dykeman was summoned and given a full report. The intelligence agent inspected the camera, then nodded to the guards. Pryce was led away, still maintaining his innocence.

The men went back to their drawing boards, and Mr Dykeman beckoned the Hardys to one side. "Could be a big break in our case."

Frank whispered, "Do you think Pryce is the security leak?"

"Good chance," the agent replied. "But we'll check out the camera for prints and see if we can find anything to indicate it held the film you boys found. Right now, we'll interrogate Pryce. Keep everything you've seen here today strictly confidential."

"Will do!" Frank agreed. "By the way, sir, have you any word from Dad?"

Mr Dykeman shook his head. "But I'm sure he'll be contacting us."

"One more question," Frank said. "Do you know Mr Orrin North?"

"North—the shipping magnate? Not personally. I understand he's prominent in town. Why?"

The Hardys told the agent of North's reward offer for finding Gomez. Mr Dykeman seemed interested but puzzled. He looked at the boys keenly. "You suspect he has an ulterior motive?"

"Yes, we do," Frank replied promptly. "We'll play along with his request and see what happens."

The boys said good-bye and left. On the way to their car they saw the Corporated Laundries truck parked near the maintenance building.

"Guess they have the concession here," said Joe.

At the gate the Hardys turned in their badges. They noticed the laundry truck behind them. It was stopped, inspected, and logged out.

"Those security guards would find a needle in a haystack!" Joe commented, as he turned into the street.

"If one is *in* the haystack," Frank quipped.

On the way home the young sleuths excitedly talked about Raymond Martin, the suspected employee Pryce, and the secret Micro-Eye project.

"Some camera!" Joe remarked. "I'll bet the Footprints gang will try anything to get it."

"Speaking of prints, I vote we return to Barren Sands right after lunch."

"Me too! That beachcomber may come back again. Let's buzz Chet."

Aunt Gertrude had plates of sizzling hamburgers and crisp French fried potatoes ready for the boys at home. They grinned in anticipation and ate hungrily.

"This hits the spot, Aunty!" Joe said.

Miss Hardy unfolded her napkin. "Glad to hear that," she remarked. "I suppose you two are up to your ears in more mysteries."

Frank laughed. "Over our heads, I'd say."

"Ran into a mystery myself today," Aunt Gertrude announced a bit smugly.

"A mystery!" Frank echoed. "Where?"

"Downtown, while I was shopping. I met Mr Ricardo."

"Mr Ricardo! You're sure?"

"Of course. I never forget a face." She paused. "But that's not all. Guess whose car he was getting into?"

Joe groaned. "I give up. Whose?"

"Mr Orrin North's," she replied. "And do you know —Mr Ricardo said he had never seen me before!"

The boys plied their aunt for details. She told them the South American had seemed uncomfortable at her greeting, brusquely insisting she had made a mistake. The two men had driven off quickly.

"The cheek of him!" she huffed. "And here I had thought he was so well-mannered!"

"Then it *was* Ricardo we chased the other day!" Frank exclaimed.

Aunt Gertrude went on indignantly, "I should have

realized there was something suspicious when he asked me on the *Capricorn* about your father."

After lunch the boys traded ideas. "Two bits says this Ricardo is in the country illegally," Frank ventured. "And another two says he's from the Huella Islands!"

"And North helped him disappear by smuggling him off the ship!" Joe exclaimed. "But why? Oh, there's the phone."

Orrin North's voice came harshly through the receiver when Joe answered. The shipowner asked if the boys had any news of the missing stowaway.

"No." At a signal from his brother, Joe added, "We have a hunch Gomez is from the Huella Islands—a refugee, maybe."

"Refugee!" North snorted. "I'm convinced he's a dangerous criminal. You boys had better nab him, and quick!"

Joe hung up, saying to Frank, "I was tempted to throw Ricardo's name at him."

"Good thing you didn't," Frank cautioned. "We'd better not show our full hand. Now let's call Chet and get out to Barren Sands!"

The Hardys had decided to reach the area before two o'clock, the time the beachcomber had arrived the day before.

Chet was waiting outside when the Hardys drove up and jumped into the car. Soon the three were heading south along the coast.

When Chet learned of his friends' trip to Micro-Eye, he looked at his pals in awe. "You really are important!" he exclaimed.

Although curious about the project, he realized that the Hardys could tell him nothing further for the present.

Half an hour later Frank parked the car in the lane leading to Barren Sands. The trio made their way swiftly through the tall grass on to the deserted beach. Soon they reached the spot where Callie had found the sea shell.

"No circle of footprints today," Joe said.

"Let's scout the rest of the beach," Frank suggested.

Farther along, the boys stopped short. A double path of fresh, damp footprints, ending at the water, led to and from a circular pattern of prints!

"Look!" Joe pointed to the circle. In the centre lay a small spiral shell.

"The same kind Callie found!" Chet observed. "Now what?"

"Get out of sight before the beachcomber shows up," Frank decided. He stooped and picked up the shell. "Come on. Let's have a look!"

The three boys backtracked, brushing over their own footprints. They hid in a sandy hollow, screened by reeds and coarse shrubs.

Frank took out his penknife. As the others watched closely, he carefully worked the small blade into the shell opening. Then he heard the crisp scratch of paper.

"Something's inside."

Slowly Frank extracted a rolled-up piece of white paper. Joe and Chet stood by breathlessly as he unfolded it.

· 13 ·

Ragged Caller

"It's a message!" Joe cried, as Frank held up the paper from the sea shell.

"What does it say?" Chet asked eagerly.

Frank read the handwritten message aloud:

> " '*To Huellas—Finally got something:*
>   *Santilla, Colombo*' "

Joe jumped at the first words.

"The Huella Islands!"

"But what could 'Santilla' and 'Colombo' mean?" Frank murmured. "They're not the names Gomez inquired about at the immigration office."

"Beats me." Chet shrugged. "Maybe they're—"

"Down! Get down—quick!"

At Joe's whispered warning they all ducked low. "Wh-who's coming?" Chet quavered.

"Sh! Sandy, the beachcomber."

Cautiously the boys peered from the hollow. The ragged figure was scuffing along the beach past their hiding place. Occasionally he stopped and looked back over his shoulder.

The boys watched intently as the man started up the slope. Reaching the top, Sandy feverishly combed through the sand near the circle of footprints.

"It's—Where is it?" he shouted, looking frantically in every direction.

Finally the beachcomber scrambled down the incline. He stopped for a moment as if trying to decide where to search, then headed for the hollow. Frank quickly pocketed the shell and the boys crouched, motionless.

They could hear the man muttering as he drew near, and the sound of bushes being slapped angrily aside. Presently the muttering ceased.

Frank raised himself stealthily and looked out. Sandy was hastening up the beach.

"Come on! Let's see where he goes!"

"Whew, that was close!" Puffing hard, Chet climbed out of the hollow behind the Hardys.

Bent low, they ran forward, keeping shielded from view by clumps of high grass. Suddenly the beachcomber veered up the beach towards the road, and the next moment dropped out of sight behind a dune. Seconds later the boys heard a car start. They raced to the top of the dune and saw a red-and-white hardtop pull away from the side of the road in the direction of Bayport.

"There he goes!" Joe cried out.

The three dashed to the convertible. Frank took the wheel and spun out of the lane after the hardtop. He kept far enough behind so that its driver would not suspect pursuit.

"That's a jazzy wagon for a beachcomber to own,"

Joe remarked. "He must get good money for his sea-shell pickups."

"I'll bet he's heading straight to the person who hired him," said Frank. "And that person must know something about the Huella Islands."

"*And* the spy plot!" Joe finished. "This note clinches it."

Chet was sceptical. "That beachcomber doesn't seem smart enough to be a spy."

"Maybe he isn't," Frank replied. "Could be he doesn't even know what's in the shells."

"You mean the gang is using Sandy as they probably did Raymond Martin," Joe said.

Frank nodded, keeping his eyes on the red-and-white car. Soon it turned into the street which ran to the centre of Bayport. The trail led through the business section of town and finally into a wealthy residential area. To the boys' surprise, their quarry turned into the drive of a hedge-bordered estate.

Frank, now a block away, pulled to the kerb and the boys hopped out. Joe pointed to a gold-lettered sign at the front of the driveway which read "North Manor."

"Orrin North's home!" he exclaimed.

Excitedly the trio hurried along the quiet street and stopped at the estate's winding drive. They saw the unkempt beachcomber rush to the front door of the brick mansion.

The boys ducked back and peered round the hedge. The door was flung open and the angry face of Orrin North appeared. "You—you fool!" he rasped. "I told you never to come here!"

He irately surveyed the grounds, then pulled the man inside and slammed the door.

"For Pete's sake!" Joe exclaimed. "North *is* tied in with the spies!"

"Apparently the shells are delivered to him at some other place," said Frank. "Wonder where."

The boys crept up to the house. The first-floor windows, high off the ground, were shut.

"Shall we take a peek in?" Joe proposed.

"Better not risk it—we can't overhear anything," Frank replied.

Chet agreed. "Come on, fellows! They might spot us."

"Wait!" Frank whispered. He went over to scrutinize a jumble of footprints in the soil beneath a side window overlooking the drive. The others joined him.

"They're probably our prints," Chet said.

"No, they're not. Look at those cracks near the front of the sole, Joe. They're just like those of the intruder at our house!"

"You're right! Think they're North's?"

"No—unless he sneaks around his own house," Frank murmured. "Whoever left these was trying to get in through that window."

The Hardys were baffled. "Which means," Joe said, "the person who took Dad's papers must also be up to something in connection with North. It doesn't make sense."

"Figure it out later," Chet said nervously. "Let's go!"

Before the boys could move, footsteps came from the rear. The three friends darted behind some ornamental evergreens in front of the house. A moment later the beachcomber shuffled down the driveway to his hardtop.

"Let's grab him!" Joe whispered impulsively.

Frank shook his head. "Not yet. We don't want to let North know we suspect him."

After Sandy had left, the young sleuths waited, wondering if Orrin North would emerge. Half an hour went by with no sign of the shipowner, so the boys returned to the convertible.

"What next?" Chet asked.

"The sea-shell note," Frank replied. "We must find out who Santilla and Colombo are."

"I'll make a wild guess," Chet offered. "They're men North wants kidnapped and shipped to the Huella Islands!"

"Not bad," Frank conceded. "One of the names could even be an alias for Gomez."

Joe took up the speculation. "Or the words 'To Huellas' could mean the note itself is to be sent there."

"In which case, the names might refer to people now on the islands," Frank reasoned. "If we only knew who wrote the note!"

"Maybe Mr Ricardo," Joe ventured. "Another puzzle—do those names belong to spies or refugees?"

The Hardys decided to report to Mr Dykeman and drove directly to Micro-Eye. Chet waited in the car outside the gate while the Hardys hastened into the agent's office. They showed him the shell, handed over the note, and gave complete details, including their suspicions of the man called Ricardo.

"Good work!" the agent said, returning the shell to

Frank. "I'll have the note analysed." He frowned. "We have records of every South American refugee in the Bayport area, but Santilla and Colombo don't ring a bell."

"Then unless they're in hiding here—they may still be on one of the islands," Joe suggested.

"Yes. Unluckily, the dictator, Posada, is not co-operative with United States Intelligence—we'll have a rugged time finding out."

"Are you going to question Orrin North?" Frank asked.

"Not at present. I suggest you boys play it cool. We'll keep a tail on him, in the hope that he'll lead us to the whole spy nest if he is guilty. But North will be doubly alert, since he knows someone else picked up the shell."

Joe asked about the suspected Micro-Eye employee, Pryce. Dykeman shook his head.

"The camera discovered in his jacket took the pictures on the film found in the torn piece of Martin's raincoat. Certain defects on that roll showed up on a fresh film we ran through. But Pryce still claims he knows nothing and we gave him a thorough grilling."

Dykeman added that the camera had revealed no fingerprints. "Of course Pryce could have worn gloves. Then, again, the camera could have been planted."

The agent had shocking news for the Hardys: Raymond Martin had disappeared.

"Disappeared!"

"Yes, in Cayenne. Martin was kept under surveillance, but nevertheless he vanished from a small hotel yesterday after he checked in."

"Spies in Cayenne may have seized him when they found out about the torn raincoat," Frank said.

The Hardys spoke of their planned flight to Cayenne with Jack Wayne. "We'll try to uncover some clues to Martin and to his captors."

"Fine. You may find out more than our department could, since you can pose better as tourists. Meantime, I'll circulate a description of Ricardo. He's here illegally, I'm sure, and for no good reason."

Back at the car, Frank handed the sea shell to Chet. "Thanks!" He grinned. "Callie and Sis will be happy."

On the way home Joe voiced another idea. "I wouldn't be surprised if the Huella Islands *are* headquarters for this Footprint gang."

Frank agreed. "I have another theory, too. We're pretty sure North smuggled Ricardo in—so he may be smuggling in spies from Cayenne, too."

Chet shifted uncomfortably. "Golly, fellows. You still want to go there?"

"You bet!" Joe replied. "And to the Huellas, if possible."

Chet heaved a sigh. "I smell trouble already."

That evening Frank and Joe packed. Aunt Gertrude hovered about them, offering a constant stream of advice and warnings.

"Don't worry, Aunty," Joe assured her. "We four will stick together down there."

Frank in turn offered his aunt a suggestion. "Aunt Gertrude, maybe you'd like to visit your friend Mrs Berter while we're gone, and compare notes on your trip."

Miss Hardy gave him a sharp look. "You think I

can't take care of myself? I'm not afraid to stay here alone, young man!"

Nevertheless she finally agreed to the idea, and made plans to leave the following day. The boys were getting ready for bed when the telephone rang. "Maybe it's Dad!" said Joe, picking up their extension phone.

The caller was Chet Morton. "Guess what!" he exclaimed. "Sis and Callie looked up that shell in a book. It's unusual all right—it's the shell of a Cayenne keyhole limpet!"

"Cayenne!" Joe repeated.

"Right. '*Diodora cayenensis*,' and it's not native to this area!"

The Hardys were excited. One more link in the chain of espionage!

Would their visit to Cayenne reveal others?

·14·

Blind River

FRANK, Joe, and Chet clambered excitedly out of a taxi at Bayport Airport the next morning. They tipped the driver and scooped their suitcases out of the boot.

"There's Jack!" Joe announced, spotting the plane at the end of a runway. The boys trotted across the field.

"All set?" the pilot greeted them.

"You bet!"

The luggage was hoisted aboard, then the Hardys and Chet climbed in. Jack swung behind the controls and turned to Chet. "How's the weather forecast, Mr Morton?"

"Doing just fine!" Chet parried. "Undercast, with blue clouds expected by dayfall."

Amidst the laughter, the propeller clacked over, then spun at top speed. The craft took off, steadily gained altitude, and levelled off at ten thousand feet. Jack said he would land it in Cayenne the following afternoon.

Then Frank asked about the repaired wing. Jack

replied, "I had her carefully checked out this morning. Also, I've been keeping a sharp lookout for visitors with machetes."

"That's a relief!" Chet said emphatically.

Joe asked Jack if he had had any leads on the luggage thefts at Cayenne.

"Only that the victims so far have come mostly from the Bayport area."

Hours passed as the plane flew south through a bright, clear sky. The boys talked about what to expect in Cayenne. At noon they brought out sandwiches and a thermos of lemonade.

Jack landed that evening at San Juan, Puerto Rico, and they spent the night at an airport motel. Shortly after sunrise they were airborne again.

"Next stop—French Guiana!" Chet mumbled as he dozed off. When he awoke later, he sat up, yawned, and squinted out of the window. Instead of endless, grey sea, lush green terrain drifted slowly beneath them.

"Wow!" Chet's eyes flew open. "Jungles!"

When the plane headed briefly out to sea, the Hardy's recognized a line of staggered islands below. "The Huellas!" Frank exclaimed. "That big one must be Baredo."

Jack banked inland over dense jungle broken only by twisting brown rivers. There seemed to be no sign of life.

When the Cayenne airfield came into view, the Bayporters fastened their seat belts. There was a wait while a jet from the Unites States landed; then Jack touched down and brought his craft to a smooth stop.

Joe pushed open the cabin door and caught his breath. It was like stepping into an oven!

Chet grimaced. "I feel like a broiled hamburger already."

The boys dropped on to the glaring, sunlit field. After Jack had handed down the baggage, they went quickly through customs.

Passengers from the jetliner thronged outside towards waiting buses and taxis. Around the small airport only wild, green jungle could be seen. The air seemed dead with heat.

A woman's shrill cry startled the boys. Frank wheeled around to see two ill-dressed, swarthy men break out of the crowd, each carrying a blue suitcase.

"Help! Help! Thief!"

"Joe! They've stolen that woman's luggage!"

Like lightning, the Hardys tore after the thieves. A police whistle shrieked. An officer fired two warning shots in the air, then joined the chase.

"*Attendez! Attendez!*"

The thieves skirted the control tower and ran across the airfield. Frank and Joe soon outdistanced the pursuing policeman. But the thieves reached the end of a runway and in a moment disappeared into the jungle.

"Come on!" Joe plunged into the thick growth. The next instant he felt a crashing blow on the head, toppled over, and lay half stunned.

"Okay, monsieur?"

"Joe! Are you all right?"

The policeman's and Frank's voices pierced a ringing blackness. Groggy, Joe was helped to his feet. "The thieves—"

"They got away," Frank told him grimly. The officer said he had tracked the men for a short distance, but lost them in a tangle of vines.

"How's your head?" Frank asked.

"It'll be all right after the ache stops. One of those lugs must have landed a suitcase on me."

The Hardys and the officer emerged from the jungle. Jack, Chet, and two more policemen joined them and they all walked back to the terminal.

Chet wiped his moist face and groaned. "I tried to catch up with you but no go."

Later, the boys and police officers spoke with the victims of the robbery, a middle-aged American couple named Griffin. Mr Griffin could not add much to the thieves' description, except that he judged them to be natives.

"Alice had expensive jewellery in her bag," he said disconsolately. His wife wept quietly.

The police were apologetic, and assured the Griffins that anyone spotted trying to sell the stolen items in Cayenne would be arrested.

Jack explained his mission to the police, who promised full co-operation. He and the boys then hailed a taxi. On the way to the city they mulled over the incident.

"Five minutes here and we're right in the thick of the luggage thefts," Jack said. "Did you know the Griffins were from Taylorville?"

"Near Bayport?" Joe asked.

"That's right."

Frank said thoughtfully, "Why are people from our area the only targets? There must be a good reason!"

Jack's plan was to confer with local airline people and try to trace possible suspects. The boys would work independently. Soon the taxi turned into a dirt road on the outskirts of Cayenne and pulled up at a modest hotel.

Chet brightened. "Civilization at last!" he rejoiced.

The four booked into comfortable rooms over-looking palm-covered slopes. Chet immediately rushed into the shower and turned on the cold water full blast. The Hardys followed in turn.

After changing into fresh clothes, the boys walked down to the centre of Cayenne. Jack had already headed back to the airport.

"Say, how about some chow?" Chet suggested.

"After we scout around," Frank said.

The boys had decided first to seek some clue to Raymond Martin's whereabouts in Cayenne. The next day they would go to Baredo. Frank inquired about transportation and learned that a launch ferried passengers to and from the island.

The trio reached the centrally located Place des Palmistes, and strolled through the cool park, shaded by towering palm trees. Botanical gardens and a sports stadium were visible to the east.

The Hardys recalled that Cayenne, populated by a mixture of peoples, lay at the mouth of the Cayenne River, which curled inland through wild, heat-drenched wilderness.

Presently the boys came to the beach, along which stretched a row of summer homes. To the north they could barely make out the forbidding Huellas. Frank and Joe looked for the *Dorado*, but the freighter was not in port.

At a restaurant, shaded by a grove of bamboo trees, the visitors stopped for fruit drinks. On the way back to town they purchased straw hats from a vendor and asked directions to the hotel from which Martin had disappeared. They found it without difficulty.

"Dykeman's already checked this place," Frank said. "But let's see what we can find out."

The young sleuths entered the dim, stuffy lobby and went up to the desk. Casually Frank asked the clerk if Mr Martin had returned. The thin-faced man looked sullen.

"I already tell everybody—he just disappear—*poof!* And not pay his bill either."

Further questioning proved futile and the boys left. "Our best bet now is to keep looking for him in town," said Joe.

Hindus, Arabs, natives, and Europeans milled past the boys. Flies buzzed at fish stands and butchers' meat stalls. Near some grey stone public buildings Chet gasped as a huge bull-like beast with curved horns clopped by hauling a cart.

"A water buffalo!" Frank exclaimed.

"If he's taking to land, I'll take to water!" Chet shuddered.

"There are piranha—flesh-devouring fish—in the river," Joe informed him challengingly.

"Flesh-devouring!" Chet's eyes bulged.

"—Not to mention centipedes, poisonous snakes, scorpions, and crocodiles in the jungle," Frank added sombrely.

The Hardys grinned as they strolled on. The Bay-porters paused beneath a handsome mahogany tree. A scar-faced vendor was hawking cheap garments at a nearby shop front. The vendor, spotting the boys, held up one piece after another.

"Pants—shirts—cheap?" he offered in broken English.

Joe shook his head. The peddler shrugged and next proffered a wrinkled white raincoat.

Suddenly Frank hastened over. "Joe! Chet! Come here!" Frank had flipped over the coat to reveal a bright plaid lining and a large jagged hole at the hem!

"Raymond Martin's raincoat!" Joe gasped.

"This hole matches the piece we found at the airport!"

Frank asked the puzzled vendor where he had obtained the coat. The man summoned a tall ear-ringed Guianan from the shop and spoke with him in rapid French.

"*La fleuve*," the peddler told the boys, pointing to the river. "Down two, three mile. You buy?"

"*Oui*." Frank brought out several francs and handed them over.

"But how will we get down the Cayenne River?" Joe whispered. "That's real jungle."

"He take you—for price," the vendor confided, motioning to the native.

Arrangements were made for the trip and the boys followed their guide towards the river. On the way Chet bought some tropical fruit.

Soon they came to a short wooden dock. Next to it was a dugout canoe with hornlike stern and bow curving upwards. The native beckoned the boys to climb in. "To coat man—I take you."

Chet was uneasy. "Do you think we can trust him?" he whispered to the Hardys.

"I think so," Frank replied. "We haven't much choice if we want to find Martin."

With Frank and the guide paddling, and Joe and Chet seated in the middle, the canoe glided out into the motionless, mud-coloured water. A searing sun burned down as they slipped past lush green jungle banks. White clouds were mirrored in the still river surface.

Presently they passed a clearing of thatch-roofed Indian huts. Farther along, several native women were beating laundry with flat sticks at the waterside. After a while the only sound was the chatter of birds from the depths of the jungle. Something in the primeval stillness prompted the boys to speak in whispers.

"It's like another world!" Joe said, awed.

Past a bend a flock of beautiful flamingos scattered at the canoe's approach. Several crocodiles lay sleepily along the banks. Chet held his breath until they had left the ugly creatures behind.

Several miles farther, the native pointed to a channel off to the right. Frank nodded and they steered in. Enormous mangrove trees arched overhead, blocking out the sun. Gnarled vines hung in trailing loops. The travellers ducked as low-hanging branches tore at their shirts and faces.

"Here!" The guide steered towards a bank covered by thick roots. The boys sat breathlessly, their hearts pounding. Were they about to meet the missing Raymond Martin?

The canoe glided against the bank, where the

Guianan pointed to a long, overhanging branch, then at the torn raincoat. Frank understood.

"He means he found the raincoat hanging from that branch!"

"A distress signal by Martin!" Chet guessed.

"The coat man—where is he?" Joe asked the guide.

The native hopped out, secured the craft, and motioned the boys to follow. They clambered after him up the bank into the jungle. Something in his expression made the boys uneasy. Was he leading them into a trap?

"Stick together," Frank cautioned Joe and Chet.

Patches of blue sky broke through the dense foliage. The guide stopped at a small clearing and the boys peered ahead at the remnants of a campfire. A laceless black shoe lay nearby.

Joe picked it up and read the faded brand name, one familiar to the boys. The clearing seemed eerily deserted. The Guianan led them to a patch of thick shrub. "Here—coat man!"

With a sweep of his arm he threw back the dropping mass of leaves, disclosing a long white form. The Hardys and Chet gasped.

A human skeleton!

· 15 ·

City of Silence

THE three boys peered, shocked at the skeleton. Frank stepped back as a centipede slithered out of the skull. Chet backed away, shuddering. "L-let's get out of here!"

The Hardys, too, had instinctively recoiled, but now inspected the skeleton more closely.

"This can't be Raymond Martin." Frank pointed out the parched discolouring and cracks in the bones. Several fragments were missing. "These are old—maybe a year or more. Look how the grass has grown around them!"

Joe also recalled their fleeting glimpse of Martin. He was a taller man than the skeleton would indicate. Frank turned to their puzzled guide and said, "Not coat man."

The native looked disappointed and shrugged. Through gestures he indicated that he knew nothing more.

The boys searched for clues. Finding none, they returned to the dugout. Joe took the bow paddle this time and they headed back upriver.

Frank said he felt that the raincoat had been left there as a trick by the person or persons who had kidnapped Martin; also, that the shoe and campfire were part of the scheme.

"You think he's still alive?" Joe asked.

"Yes, though it's just a hunch. Spies may be holding him to find out what happened to their missing Micro-Eye film."

"Or to keep him from telling Dykeman's men how the film got into his coat—if he even knows that," Joe ventured.

Chet had a guess. "Maybe they sneaked into his house the way the intruder did at Dad's travel agency," Chet suggested.

Frank snapped his fingers. "If he wanted the names of persons flying to Cayenne, maybe Martin *was* to be a victim of the luggage thieves—only they planned to take his coat instead of his suitcase."

Chet whistled. "Then the suitcases stolen down here may carry spy messages?"

"That's right—brought in by innocent people."

A sudden wind came up and the bright blue skies turned to a smoky leaden hue. The paddlers increased speed and reached the dock at Cayenne just as the clouds opened in a blinding downpour.

The boys and their guide leaped ashore and dashed to a nearby shop for shelter. Torrents of rain drummed on the roof like thunder, and the tall coconut palms swayed and bent in the gale.

"Chet, you didn't forecast this cloudburst," Joe needled.

"How could I? Tropical storms come up out of nowhere!" Chet defended himself.

In several minutes the squall ceased as suddenly as it had begun. Frank paid their guide, who grinned widely and ambled off. The boys walked back through the town to their hotel, where they dried off and once more changed clothes.

Refreshed, the boys joined Jack at supper in the hotel restaurant. He listened with interest as they recounted their adventure in low tones. When Frank presented his theory on the luggage thefts, the pilot was intrigued.

"It's possible," he admitted, frowning, "that travellers from Bayport and nearby towns unwittingly transmit Micro-Eye secrets. But how are the films or devices put into the suitcases?"

"We're not sure yet," Joe confessed. "Somebody probably sneaks into the person's home and conceals the information in the baggage."

"Could be," said Frank.

"My conferences today didn't bring me any clues," Jack told the boys. "But if you're right, fellows, this is a job for United States Intelligence. I'll case Cayenne tomorrow, myself, and try to follow out this new angle. We'll have to fly back the day after."

The Hardys reviewed what they must learn: the real identity of Gomez, the meaning of the names in the sea shell, some clue to North's tie-in with the Huellas, and the whereabouts of Martin.

"It'll be a tight schedule," Frank said. "We'll catch the earliest launch for Baredo tomorrow morning."

Jack said, "Let's report to Mr Dykeman."

He cabled the intelligence officer, using guarded language. Later, as they again discussed the mystery, Jack expressed concern over the boys' proposed trip to Baredo.

"Be extremely cautious," he warned. "Dictator Posada has lookouts all over the place."

At his suggestion the boys signed a statement that they were entering Baredo the following day. "At least this will be evidence if we're—er—detained," said Frank, handing the paper to Jack.

"What a cheerful thought!" Chet muttered.

The young sleuths soon went to bed, and despite the sultry heat, slept soundly. Chet had a nightmare. He was trying to step into the river for a swim, but hungry fish nipped his toes.

Suddenly he awakened with a violent start. Something was on his right foot! He reached down and touched a furry object.

"*YYYYoooowwwww!*"

At Chet's howl the others leaped out of bed, and Joe switched on the light. Chet was hopping up and down, shaking his foot. A dark winged creature flew out the window.

Jack examined Chet's foot and smiled with relief. "No blood. Fortunately, you shook him off in time. I think it was a vampire bat."

"A v-vampire b-bat?" Chet clapped a hand to his brow. "Oh man! That's all I need!" With a groan he got back into bed and wrapped himself tightly in the sheet.

The boys rose at six and breakfasted quickly downstairs. Then they walked to the coastal docks. Frank said he had promised Jack they would be back by ten that evening.

Chet, apprehensive, followed the Hardys to the dock where the tourist launch was berthed. The boys were met by a fat, thick-lipped man in uniform, evidently a Huellan official.

"American tourists?" he said, sneering. "You go just for day to Baredo?"

"Yes."

The official scrutinized the travellers, then their passports. "Very well," he said finally. "See you mind your own business and no pictures."

"Friendly guy," Chet whispered, as the boys climbed aboard.

The whistle blew and a few minutes later the launch moved away towards the mist-covered Huellas. There were no other passengers.

The thickset helmsman and his assistant were taciturn. After a sharp glance at the boys they paid them no further attention.

The Hardys and Chet stood at the rail as they approached the palm-lined shore of Baredo. A hill of green jungle rose above the roofs of the capital town. Was their destination the stronghold of the Footprints spy ring?

The boat's whistle tooted three times, and chugged into the harbour. This consisted of several weather-beaten piers and a few small docks. The launch pulled alongside one of them.

When the boys clambered on to the dock, the helmsman grunted, "Up there." He pointed to a small guard-house at the foot of the dock. Here a surly port officer studied their passports at length. "Tourists only allowed on Baredo one day!" he snapped. "You must leave tonight!"

"*Gracias*," Frank murmured, and the trio headed up the bleak main street.

"With that kind of welcome, they must do a crashing resort business here," Joe remarked.

The boys had noticed numerous motorboats marked *Policia* cruising about the island, apparently to control passage out of the Huellas.

"No wonder the people here want to leave," Chet whispered.

Impressive public buildings fronted the harbour. But in the town itself the boys saw rows of tottering, unpainted shacks along unpaved roads. Shabbily dressed people wandered past dingy stores, many of which appeared to be closed. The atmosphere was both tense and depressing.

"Boy, this place gives me the willies," Chet murmured, as he noticed a grey-uniformed man watching them from one of the few cars.

"Never mind. Let's just try to look like happy tourists," Joe advised.

They climbed to the top of a hill outside town and surveyed the harbour. Only their launch and a battered fishing vessel were tied up.

Frank's eyes narrowed. "It would be impossible for a big freighter to dock here."

"You mean like the *Dorado*," Joe said.

His brother nodded, then suggested they try to track down the names Colombo and Santilla, and also ask about Gomez.

Back in town, the boys located a rickety public telephone booth. Casually Frank entered it and opened a thin directory. None of the names he sought was listed. "There can't be more than a hundred or so names in here," he reported. "I guess most of the citizens can't afford phones, or else Posada's tight on giving them out."

"Doesn't leave us much of a starting point," Joe said. "Let's try asking around."

They stopped an elderly man and mentioned the three names, but he shrugged, stared blankly, and walked away. The boys continued their quest. But they always met the same response.

"Let's try a different part of town," Joe recommended. They headed into a small market place and made more inquiries without success.

"Colombo, Santilla—Gomez?" Frank repeated to a poorly dressed boy.

The youth's expression stiffened. He shook his head and quickly hurried off.

"I don't get it," Joe fumed. "Are the people so afraid of something that they won't talk at all? Or is there something special about Colombo, Santilla, and Gomez that scares them?"

"It's the secret police!" Chet declared uneasily. "Why else would everybody clam up?"

The boys noticed another man in a grey uniform striding past. He eyed the boys suspiciously. The trio immediately pretended to be sightseeing. Chet whistled shakily as they nonchalantly left the market place.

"We'd better call it quits for a while," Frank whispered. "And—" He broke off. "Look!"

Crossing the main street, not far from the boys, were two men carrying blue suitcases.

"The luggage thieves!" Joe gasped.

"Come on! We're going to find out where they're heading!" Frank urged.

· 16 ·

The Gate of Doom

THE Hardys and Chet walked faster, keeping the two thieves in sight. When the men turned swiftly up a hilly, sun-baked street, the boys paused briefly at the corner, then followed.

"Wherever they're going, they mean business!" Frank said.

The men hastened up the hill. At the top they made a beeline to a large white stone building, surrounded by a spiked iron fence with a huge gate in front. The pair stopped and spoke briefly to an armed guard, who let them in. The men hurried through and disappeared round the side of the building.

"There's probably a rear entrance," Joe murmured, as the guard slammed the gate shut.

The boys approached the building. Carved over the portal was : EDIFICIO ADMINISTRATIÓN DE LAS HUELLAS

"Huellas Government Building!" Frank translated. "And I'll bet a cool shower it adds up to 'Footprints Intelligence Bureau'!"

"The spy headquarters!" Joe added in a low voice.

A chill went up Chet's spine. "You think those men really are delivering Micro-Eye secrets hidden in the suitcases?" he asked.

"Yes," Frank replied. "This must be the receiving end for the security leak at the plant!"

The Hardys speculated about the two thieves—were they Colombo and Santilla? Noticing the guard, who eyed them with mistrust, the boys sauntered nonchalantly towards the rear of the building.

"Where do we go from here?" Joe asked. "We can't break in."

Chet agreed heartily. "And we sure can't hang around waiting for those spy agents."

At his urging they stopped at a dingy restaurant to have lunch. But the trio felt too edgy to eat much. Back outside, the afternoon sun burned down on the perspiring boys. Two oxcarts rolled lazily down the dusty street.

"If only we could get some lead on these names!" Joe chafed. "Time's running out."

The trio walked on to a section they had not visited before—consisting mostly of small shops and rickety dwellings. The three separated in order to appear less conspicuous while they continued their inquiries. After an hour they met. Each reported no luck.

Just then the boys noticed a dark, well-built man in khakis resting beneath a palm tree across the road. They went over and Frank once more repeated the three names. The Huellan's eyes focused intently on his questioner, then studied Joe and Chet.

"*No, lo siento,*" he said finally, quickly moving away. He looked back once, then disappeared into a ramshackle store.

"At least we got an answer," Joe said wryly. "He's 'sorry.'"

"He didn't act frightened like the others," Frank observed. "I have a feeling he knew the names, all right, and was trying to size us up."

They renewed their inquiries. But after another sweltering hour, the boys had reached a dead end. They had covered the town itself, and now found themselves on the western outskirts.

"I'm ready to throw in the towel," Chet announced. "This is no man's land."

The Hardys did not reply. They had noticed the door of a small building slowly opening. A face peered out. It was the same khaki-clad man Frank had approached earlier!

"Maybe he's tailing us!" Joe whispered.

The stranger stared at the boys for a second, then suddenly burst outside and sprinted for the nearby jungle. Joe and Frank sped after him, with Chet following reluctantly.

In minutes the boys found themselves on the bare semblance of a trail. There was no sign of the Huellan.

"He's probably waiting to jump us!" Chet declared.

Frank set his jaw. "Let's follow this trail. It may be risky, but we can't give up any possible lead."

The three were forced to proceed single file. Progress was slow and arduous over twisting roots and through masses of hanging vine. A dense cloud of mosquitoes enveloped them, attacking Chet in particular.

"Ouch!" *Swat!* "Get away from me!" Chet flailed desperately at the buzzing pests.

"*Ssssh!*"

"I can't help it. They're eating me up."

Frank, in the lead, stopped abruptly and held up his hand. There came a faint rustling ahead. Cautiously the boys crept round a bend in the trail. To their surprise, a large section of jungle was hacked away. In the middle was an abandoned quarry.

"Looks like an old bauxite deposit," Frank whispered.

Chet pointed to several rusted pickaxes on the ground. "Wonder what happened to the workers." He shuddered.

The boys skirted the yawning pit, treading over crumbling red rock, then re-entered the jungle. There was still a barely perceptible path. The high grass growing along it was freshly trampled.

"Bet that guy's right ahead of us," Joe said softly. "He must be used to trekking the jungle."

Chet was all for turning back, but the Hardys persuaded him to press on. The trail ended abruptly at a high, crudely constructed stucco wall. Farther along it was an arched gateway with a faded splintered sign: LA PUERTA DE LA MUERTE.

" '*The Gate of Doom*'!" Joe translated. "The old prison!"

Reluctantly Chet trailed the Hardys along the wall and through the gateway. Interspersed among towering bamboo trees which blotted out most of the sunlight were long, thatch-roofed shacks.

"Probably the old prison barracks," Frank whispered. "That man may be hiding out in one."

They advanced cautiously, catching occasional glimpses through the foliage of the encircling wall. Lonely bird caws echoed around the deserted compound. The air hung hot and still. Pickaxes and broken machetes littered the ground. Looking up, the boys saw several ugly vultures hunched in the trees.

Chet gulped. "Ugh!"

The trio paused behind a bamboo tree, then slipped between two shacks facing a large clearing. In the centre of this stood a platform and on top of it was a guillotine.

Chet stood rooted to the spot, quaking with fright. Frank pointed to a shack across the clearing. At his signal the boys darted over to it and crouched low. A trail of footprints ended beneath the single small window.

"They're fresh!" Joe whispered.

The boys crept to the window and Joe slowly rose to peer inside. His eyes had just reached the window level when gasps from the others made him spin around.

A dozen armed, grim-faced men in khaki stood spread out in the clearing.

"Don't try to run," Frank said in an undertone. "Act calm."

"Oh, s-sure," Chet stammered, white as a sheet.

The men advanced threateningly. Some wore bandoliers and battered straw hats, and several carried gleaming machetes. Among them the boys recognized the man they had pursued. The Hardys felt a cold chill of terror, but stood outwardly calm.

Were these men soldiers of Dictator Posada? An older, bearded man with a military bearing stepped forward and uttered a brisk command in Spanish.

The boys were marched off towards the guillotine! Chet's knees almost buckled, but he relaxed as the

Bayporters were led past the gruesome platform and into an isolated shack. The first objects they saw were cots and old leg irons which were attached to a centre bar running the length of the hot, dusty room.

The Hardys and Chet were prodded to a wooden table. Lighting a paraffin lantern, the bearded man sat down and addressed the prisoners brusquely in English.

"Who are you? What is your business here?"

Frank hesitated. He must choose his words carefully!

"We're Americans, just visiting here for the day. I'm Frank Hardy, this is my—"

"Americans—" The man's steely eyes relaxed for a moment, then tightened. "You ask in town for Colombo, Santilla, Gomez. Why?"

"We don't really know," Frank said. "We came across the names in our town of Bayport and thought—"

"Names—in Bayport!"

The leader's astonished exclamation was accompanied by a rapid stream of excited Spanish conversation among his followers.

"Do *you* know the three men?" Joe spoke up.

"My friend who led you here is Carlos Santilla," the bearded man replied. "I am Miguel Colombo."

Despite their dangerous position, Frank pressed further. "Are you under orders from Dictator Posada?"

Suddenly the table rocked under Colombo's fist. "Posada—that mercenary spy—that tyrant robber of our people? *No!* We of the underground will unseat him one day!"

The men roared approval.

Frank shot a look of relief at Joe and Chet. An underground movement! They were among friends!

Colombo and Santilla then shook the boys' hands cordially.

"I am sorry for your unpleasant reception," said Colombo, "but we have always to be careful."

"Then you thought *we* might be working for Posada?" Frank asked.

Santilla nodded. "One is always afraid these days in the Huellas. That is why the lips are closed in town. If Posada knew we meet here, he would send his army to crush us!"

Colombo then directed one of his men to go outside and stand guard. "We do not wish to be caught by surprise," the leader said. "Posada's soldiers often search the jungle."

Joe asked the Huellans whether or not the dictator *was* the power behind the Footprints ring.

"Indeed he is." The leader leaned forward. "But I am troubled. My name, Santilla's—how do you young men learn these? And what do you know of Gomez?"

Omitting confidential details, the Hardys related the events which had led them to Baredo.

"And in that sea shell, you found my name and Santilla's?" he murmured.

"Yes," Frank answered. "Later, a beachcomber led us to the house of a rich American in Bayport. We suspect this man to be involved in the Footprints plot. His name is North."

"North! Orrin North?"

"Yes, the shipowner. You've heard of him?"

"Heard of him!" The bearded leader of the underground held up his hands with pride. "Señor North is our greatest ally!"

· 17 ·

Homestretch

THE Hardys and Chet could scarcely believe Colombo's words. Orrin North—an ally!

"Then North is not in league with Posada—but is in your underground movement?" Frank asked.

"Certainly. For months he has helped our people to escape on his ship *Dorado* to America."

Joe looked at Frank. "So Gomez isn't a spy!"

"No," Colombo said. "He is one of our best men, sent to rally American support. Days back, he by himself escaped to North's ship. But from what you say, he is in bad trouble."

Carlos Santilla's face showed alarm. "Something is wrong! These people Gomez asked about at your immigration office are Huellan refugees who escaped earlier on Señor North's *Dorado*!"

"They never reached the immigration office!" Joe exclaimed.

Colombo walked to the window, stunned. "It cannot be!"

"Have you heard from any of the refugees since they escaped?" Frank asked.

"No. For a while we thought it is because of Posada's

mail censorship. But now," Colombo added gloomily, "I am not so sure."

The Hardys and Chet exchanged looks. Their suspicions of Orrin North were confirmed!

"North is double-crossing you!" Joe burst out.

Colombo and Santilla stared in shocked disbelief. "He deceives us?" Santilla said hoarsely.

"Señor Colombo," countered Frank, "have any of your men been arrested lately by Posada's police?"

"*Sí*, two last week," Colombo said grimly. "We do not know how Posada found them out."

It was the answer Frank had dreaded. "I think I do —from the Footprints spies! North got the names for Posada from the refugees."

"And Gomez must have found out about it on the *Dorado*—that's why he jumped ship," Joe added.

"But," Colombo protested, "our compatriots would never betray us!"

"They may have been tricked into revealing the names!" Frank said.

The leader's face was pale. "Posada may have ordered them—to be killed!"

The Hardys did not agree. "I think it's more likely they're prisoners, and that North will ship them back for Posada to deal with!" Frank turned to Chet and Joe. "We've got to find those refugees before it's too late!"

Joe said, "That explains why Gomez wanted to keep out of sight—to find the refugees North has sold out."

Santilla relayed the boys' words in Spanish to the other men, who had been looking on intently. Angry mutters ran through the group.

The boys learned that Colombo and his lieutenant did not know about Raymond Martin or the luggage thefts. But at Joe's description of the mysterious Mr Ricardo, they both gasped.

"Manuel Bedoya is his real name!" Colombo almost shouted. "He is the feared mastermind of Posada's spies."

"You're sure?"

"Positive! We know Bedoya left the Huellas a week past." The underground chief added sombrely, "He is a dangerous and cruel man. It is not good for your government's secret project, *amigos*!"

"But why would the small Huellas be after the Micro-Eye secret?" Chet wondered. "Doesn't figure."

Joe had a theory. "Maybe to sell the information to a larger power—as part of a deal."

Colombo agreed, adding that Posada was known to be friendly with certain anti-American regimes.

Suddenly the lookout came bursting into the cabin and spoke rapidly to his leader. Colombo scowled and extinguished the lantern.

"Everyone be silent!" he commanded.

The Bayporters and the Huellans obeyed. Voices could be heard faintly in the distance, then they died away. The chief relighted the lantern.

"Who was that?" Joe asked.

"Posada's men," Santilla replied.

A few more minutes elapsed in tense waiting, but there was no further disturbance. Colombo then bade the visitors relax, and had simple rations of bread and dried beef served for supper. The boys ate hungrily. When they finished, it was growing dark.

"We have to get back," said Frank, remembering their promise to Jack.

Colombo, Santilla, and two other Huellans led the boys through a jungle route towards the docks. The hot tropical night was silent, speckled by fireflies. Miguel Colombo and his aide stopped at the jungle's edge. They thanked the boys fervently for their support.

"But what about you and Señor Santilla?" Frank asked in concern.

"We shall be all right," Colombo assured them, smiling. "We shall soon escape to the mainland. But one day we will return triumphant."

After hearty handshakes with their new friends, the boys hurried to board the waiting launch.

"I'd like to get my hands on that skunk North right now!" Joe muttered, with fierce resolution.

"We will," Frank declared. "But we've also got to find Gomez and stop Bedoya's plot against Micro-Eye!"

In relief the boys finally stepped off the launch in Cayenne. At the hotel Jack Wayne listened to their story in amazement. "So Posada may be behind these suitcase thefts," he exclaimed, "and be selling the smuggled information to a major power hostile to the United States!"

Jack whistled. "You fellows have done the work of a squadron. Ready to fly back tomorrow?"

"You bet!" Chet gingerly touched his mosquito-bitten face.

Jack reported that he had uncovered no leads to Raymond Martin, but that Dykeman's men would continue the search in French Guiana.

After a satisfying night's sleep, the four reached the airport early the next morning. As Jack loomed into the sun, the boys looked back at the trail of green islands. Could they find, and save, Colombo's missing friends?

Following an overnight stop, they landed in Bayport the next afternoon. The Hardys found Aunt Gertrude back home from her visit. She sighed with relief at seeing her nephews safe.

"Thank goodness!" she gasped. "The newspapers are full of Posada's villainous threats."

She informed the boys that Mrs Hardy would be home in a week. There was still no clue to the whereabouts of their father.

"But that rude Mr North!" she fumed. "Somehow he found out that I was at Mrs Berter's. He phoned me there and demanded to know where you boys were!"

"Did you tell him?" Frank queried.

"I should say not!"

After unpacking, Frank and Joe decided to inform Mr Dykeman at once about their trip. On their way to Micro-Eye the brothers stopped at Corporated Laundries and Joe took in a bundle of soiled clothing. As he was leaving the counter, he noticed a man with thick eyebrows in the back working room who seemed familiar.

"Funny," he mused. "I have a feeling I've seen him recently somewhere else, yet something's different."

At the Micro-Eye gate the Hardys were quickly admitted, and escorted to the intelligence office. Roy Dykeman welcomed them cordially.

"Glad to see you back! Mr Wayne's report of your

theory about spies smuggling secrets in luggage may break our case wide open!"

Mr Dykeman listened attentively as the brothers related all that had happened in Cayenne and in the Huellas. At hearing the information on Orrin North and Manuel Bedoya, the intelligence officer grabbed a pencil and jotted down notes.

"Posada's master spy—on our soil!" he exclaimed. "He must have been whisked off Orrin North's *Capricorn*!"

"Can North be arrested now?" Joe asked.

"No. We don't have an ounce of tangible proof yet. He's acted clean as a whistle since we've been watching him. But more important, we want to get the whole bunch without risking the lives of these missing Huellans!"

"How about Bedoya, alias Ricardo?" Frank asked.

"I'm sending out an alert to find him at all costs— also to apprehend Captain Burne and crew immediately in South America."

The agent reported that Gomez's whereabouts were not known, and the Micro-Eye leak was still a mystery. His men failed to locate the United States headquarters for the Footprints conspiracy.

"Pryce may be our man," he admitted, "though I'm not convinced of it. At any rate, we've reached the homestretch. Micro-Eye's satellite camera was completed this morning!"

The project was finished! Frank and Joe were elated. The top-secret instrument was to be moved under heavy protection to Washington late the following day.

"We don't want anybody to get wind of it," Dykeman added, "so we're running the usual guard shifts and concession deliveries. Once that camera is on the truck, Micro-Eye's problems are over." He gave a dry chuckle. "But not mine!"

The Hardys vowed to continue their search for Gomez, but the agent cautioned them: "Wherever Gomez is, the Footprints gang is looking for him too. Until we have Bedoya, be very careful!"

Frank and Joe gave their assurances and drove home. The boys enjoyed a delicious dinner, but all the while were trying to figure out a way to track down Gomez. Later Chet arrived and insisted that they drive out with him to Oak Hollow. The damage to the houses had been repaired.

"Dad says Mr Prito's men finished and left after supper tonight," Chet said, as they rattled along in his jalopy. "Occupancy in a week!"

It was dusk when the boys reached Oak Hollow. They parked and got out to survey the houses at close range. The hacked doors and windows and broken windows had been completely replaced.

Frank looked puzzled. "It still beats me why those machete fellows picked on this place."

The night watchman strolled by with a wave, then the trio walked to the rear of one house. It overlooked the valley, now in black shadows except for brilliant patches of moonlight.

"Nice view," Joe observed.

Suddenly the boys saw a clump of bushes stir below them to the left. A man's face looked out, then vanished.

Gomez!

"Wait!" Frank yelled.

They rushed down to the bushes. But there was only silence. Frank called Gomez's name several times. No response.

"It's useless," Chet muttered. "He has probably fled into the woods."

Just then, through a grove of trees to their right, Joe spotted several upright white objects. "Come on!"

The others followed him through the grove, emerging at the foot of a grassy hillock. Frank bumped into an iron fence before he recognized the objects as gravestones. "The cemetery!"

Finding the gate, the boys slipped through and crouched near a large gravestone. Was Gomez hiding somewhere within the cemetery itself? At the top of the slope stood a square building with no windows and a single door of bronze and glass. Chet shuddered. "A mausoleum."

"This must be a private cemetery," Frank whispered. "But what's Gomez doing around here?"

"W-what are we doing around here? Let's go!" Chet begged.

"Nothing doing. If Gomez is here, it's for a reason."

Suddenly Frank felt Chet tug at his arm. "What is it?" he asked.

The chunky youth pointed up the slope, his eyes glazed with fear. His words would hardly come.

"Th-that tomb up th-there! The d-door is opening!"

A Sinister Meeting

As if hypnotized, the three boys watched the tomb. Slowly its metal door opened wider.

They froze as a tall, shadowy figure emerged and walked in long strides to the edge of the hill. The boys crouched lower. Chet tried to swallow the lump of fear in his throat.

The gaunt figure stood in ghostly silhouette. There was no mistaking the dark-spectacled, hawk-nosed profile.

Manuel Bedoya!

The three boys were dumfounded. Had he actually appeared from the tomb! Or were they seeing things?

"He's no ghost!" Joe whispered finally.

The spy appeared to be waiting for someone. He glanced frequently at his wrist.

Moonlight painted the cemetery in an eerie, silvery glow. As the boys huddled behind the large gravestone, Joe squinted to make out its inscription. He nudged the others. They gaped at the name beneath the birth and death dates:

JAMES NORTH

"This might be Orrin North's private family

cemetery! Maybe James was his father."

"And North lets the gang hide out in the tomb!" Frank exclaimed. "That would explain the Oak Hollow sabotage."

"To keep people from occupying the houses!" Chet added, "until—"

The boys spoke in whispers, keeping an eye on Bedoya. Soon they heard faint voices from beyond the cemetery. The gaunt spy disappeared down the other side of the slope.

"He's meeting someone!" Frank said.

"Now's our chance!" Joe urged. "If they go inside the tomb, we'll never hear anything."

Chet gulped. "You m-mean *we* go inside?"

"Yes!"

"But—but somebody else may be in there," Chet objected. "We'd better get the police!"

"Bedoya might leave in the meantime," said Frank. "Even if two of us stayed, there'd be no car to follow him. I say we chance it!"

They looked up the hill at the half-opened tomb door. A red glow from within was visible. The boys decided that one of them should remain as lookout at the gravestone. Frank turned to Chet. "Would you rather wait here?"

"Alone? Not on your life!"

"I'll stay," Joe offered.

Frank and Chet started cautiously up the slope. Chet, his heart pounding, kept close at Frank's heels. At the top Frank paused, then broke for the tomb. Reaching it, he signalled Chet, who quickly followed. They peered round one corner towards the rear.

Voices still drifted up from below. There was not a sound from inside.

"Okay, here goes!"

Frank slipped through the door, then Chet. They stopped and looked around the square, stone chamber.

The air in the vault was dead and musty. In the middle of the room stood a wooden table strewn with newspapers in Spanish. The reddish glow came from a paraffin lamp on the table. Several machetes lay near a locker stocked with canned foods. A small short-wave set stood in one corner.

"The last place anybody'd suspect of being a hide-out," Frank murmured. "But no Gomez, or Huellan refugees."

Voices could be heard approaching. "Bedoya's coming back!" Chet quavered. "And he's not alone!"

It was too late for the boys to slip out unseen! They looked desperately around for a hiding place. Frank's keen eyes spotted a small descending spiral stairway in the shadows.

"Down here!"

Quickly the boys swung down the metal steps, Chet first. Frank's head dropped below floor level just as the first man entered the tomb. The two boys crouched tensely.

In a moment a jumble of voices echoed from above, some speaking in Spanish, others in English. The talking died down as the heavy door clanked shut. Chet's throat went dry, and Frank felt a twinge of fear. Below them, they discerned several cots in the dimness, but no sign of any prisoners.

"Good evening, gentlemen," said a suave, accented

voice. "Everyone accounted for? *Bueno*. Let us begin."

The voice was undoubtedly Bedoya's! It continued:

"Everything is ready to carry out Posada's order—to get the satellite camera at all costs. By eight tomorrow morning, Dykeman's precautions will have been for nothing and our Footprints mission completed!"

"Not soon enough for me," a gruff voice commented. "I'm sick of this bone house!"

Frank caught his breath. A plot to steal the government camera itself—tomorrow!

"Never mind that," the first voice said coldly. "Decker, will 41 be offshore for delivery at the given time?"

"Precisely. I reached them by radio from the *Northerly* two hours ago. There will be room for all of you."

"Good. We cannot fail! With this fool Pryce under suspicion, the plant may have false confidence in their security. Are your plans set, Valdez?"

"*Sí*. The smoke bombs are ready. We will knock out the guards. Mr North has two cars for us—Rodriguez and I will take one, while Greber and Walton will use the other."

A voice that sounded vaguely familiar to Frank added, "The uniforms are ready, Señor Bedoya. The change will take only an instant."

Frank racked his brain. Where *had* he heard the voice before? Carefully he mounted the steps until he could just see into the vault.

Bedoya, alias Ricardo, wearing a white suit, stood at one end of the table, encircled by seven men. Hunched over the flickering red lantern, Posada's chief spy seemed poised like a vulture. Frank looked over the rest of the group.

Of three, ill-kempt, swarthy men, he recognized two as those who had vandalized the Oak Hollow houses. One must be Rodriguez. The third was the stocky man with sideburns—Valdez.

The huge, bushy-haired thug, Walton, was present, and a short, bald man whom Frank also recognized— the impostor who had tried to arrest Gomez.

To Bedoya's left, near the door, sat the pilot of North's yacht. "He must be Decker," Frank reasoned, "since he has the 'offshore' job."

The boy's attention was finally riveted on a thin, heavy-browed man speaking at the opposite end of the table. His was the voice Frank had recalled hearing before.

The man complained, "This luggage business has been too sticky—and now we find out from the boss those blueprints we photographed were phonys!"

"That camera will be no phony," Bedoya remarked gloatingly. "You are sure it will fit into our waterproof bag, Al?"

"Certain of it," was the reply.

Suddenly Frank visualized a moustache on Al's clean-shaven face and stiffened. Of course!

"He's the guard who stopped Joe and me near the plant's maintenance building on our tour!" Frank recalled. "He's the Micro-Eye security leak. We must stop them!"

Bedoya and his henchmen spoke for some time in Spanish. Frank caught the name "Martin" several times. Now the chief spy leaned forward.

"One unpleasant item," he said, raising his voice. "I received word tonight that those meddling sons of Fenton Hardy went to Baredo seeking Gomez, and two subversives, both of whom I regret to say escaped to French Guiana. Posada is not pleased."

The men muttered uneasily. Chet had crept up behind Frank. The two boys felt a surge of joy. Colombo and Santilla had got away!

"Those young punks," Walton growled. "Too bad Greber and Valdez and me didn't finish 'em off at the boathouse."

Bedoya's lips curled scornfully. "You were all fools to muff the chance!"

"Next time I get my hands on the Hardy pests and their fat friend—" Walton clenched and unclenched his huge fists. Chet felt a trickle of sweat running down his brow.

There was a sudden sharp cry from outside the tomb. Manuel Bedoya straightened up. "That was Jose! He must have caught somebody snooping!"

An icy chill went through Frank and Chet. Was Joe in the enemy's clutches? The next instant Bedoya doused the lantern and the eight men rushed outside.

"Chet! Come on!"

Frank whipped up the stairway and leaped for the closing tomb door, but too late. It clanked firmly shut! Frantically the boys pushed against it to no avail. They were sealed in!

Chet gasped. "We'll never get out alive!"

Frank noticed a fine slot near the door handle. "Bedoya must have had a key!"

Suddenly a click sounded from outside, and the door

began to open. The two boys braced themselves for battle.

"It's all right—it's me!"

"Joe!"

"Thank heavens!" Chet sighed, faint with relief.

Frank started to speak, but his brother motioned them out of the tomb. In the woods to their right, the boys could hear a commotion of voices. They circled to the back of the vault and ran down the slope into a clump of pine trees.

"They've—got—Gomez," Joe panted.

"What?"

"Yes. Bedoya had two guards hidden near the cemetery. I saw Gomez a second before they captured him. The others rushed out of the tomb before I could do anything!"

"Joe, they've hatched a plot to get the Micro-Eye camera tomorrow morning!" Quickly Frank recounted all they had heard. "We've got to tell Dykeman—but we can't leave Gomez helpless!"

The boys listened intently. Now only silence met their ears. Swiftly and silently, the Hardys and Chet circled the cemetery. Still no sounds, or sign of anyone.

"Funny," Joe muttered. "I didn't hear a car start up."

Chet again urged that they go for the police.

"Guess we'll need help," Frank agreed. "And we have to warn Micro-Eye!"

They pushed through the dark woods, Chet ploughing ahead like a tank in a thicket. "Boy, am I glad to get out of here!"

Joe had just started up the rise towards the housing development when a beam of light flashed out from the right. Then another! To their left, still another!

"Look out!"

Before the boys could retreat, rough arms seized all three from behind. Frank and Joe bucked and kicked at the men holding them. Joe grimaced with pain as his captor applied a vicious arm lock. Frank, helpless in a choking grip, saw Chet had been thrown to the ground after a valiant struggle against two assailants.

The boys, hopelessly outnumbered, were gagged and dragged a short distance. Frank was first to sight the limp, gagged form of Gomez at the feet of a white-suited figure.

Manuel Bedoya's voice uttered one menacing word. "Strike!"

The next instant blows crashed upon the boys' heads. They sank down, unconscious!

· 19 ·

Ghost Ship

SLOWLY Joe revived. His arms were bound tightly behind his back.

He felt the steady throb of a motor and a rocking motion. As a splash of water hit his face, he sat up but fell back as a strong gust of salty wind hit him. Joe now realized he was in the stern of a boat moving at top speed through the darkness.

Frank and Chet, also tied up, lay inert on deck next to him. As a wave leaped the rail and doused them, they both sat up groggily.

Frank winced. "My head—where are we?"

Joe whispered, looking around, "I think we're aboard the *Northerly*!"

Two Huellan thugs, whom the boys recognized as the machete men, glared at the trio from the taffrail. Nearby lay the unconscious form of Gomez. To starboard, the boys could just see the mainland. They were heading south, but where?

The Hardys strained futilely against their bonds. Prisoners! And a sinister spy scheme to be executed against Micro-Eye within a few hours!

"Watch the rocks!" a voice called out. The boys

spotted Bedoya standing on the bridge above. Chet's teeth chattered.

Presently the yacht turned in a slow arc, then the engines stopped. The *Northerly*'s lights were cut, except one beam to the fore.

The shoreline was in complete blackness. Suddenly, ahead, the three boys made out a huge, hulking outline. They drew closer to the enormous shadow.

Frank gasped. "The *Atlantis*!"

Moments later, the captives were rudely pulled to their feet and untied. The Huellan, Rodriguez, prodded them with a blunt instrument.

"One sound and you are finished."

In grim silence the Hardys and Chet were thrust into a dinghy with one man at the oars; then Gomez, still unconscious, was lifted in. The two thugs climbed in and the oarsman pushed off. Bedoya and his other henchmen followed in a second boat.

The two craft made directly for the old wreck. Nearer and nearer it loomed, until the tilted hull hovered over them. A rope ladder was lowered from the port side.

"Up!" Rodriguez ordered the captive youths.

Frank, Joe, and Chet gripped the swaying ladder and climbed to the freighter's deck. The three men seized and handcuffed them.

Chet crouched against the strong wind, trying desperately to keep his balance on the slanted deck. A shaft of light pierced the darkness as one of the men opened a hatch.

"Down there!" he barked.

The trio obeyed, with their captors following. Below,

the boys were led aft through a dim passageway lined with broken rusted piping to an open doorway. Here an olive-skinned muscular man yanked the boys inside.

They found themselves in a large compartment, illuminated dimly by several lanterns. Cots and chairs were scattered about. A battered desk stood near a rack of rifles. On the desk lay a crate of fruit, several sea shells of the keyhole limpet variety, and a riding crop.

The boys' attention was quickly drawn to a group of weary-looking people seated on blankets at the rear of the hold. The eight men and three women looked Latin American. Their wrists and ankles bound, they seemed too exhausted to show much surprise at the new arrivals.

One of the men moaned. Seeing lash marks across his face, Frank grimaced. "The Huellan refugees!" he whispered. "Thank heavens they're alive!"

"Not by much!" Joe commented, appalled. "Bedoya must have them beaten. I wonder how long they've been kept here."

"Weeks, probably," Frank estimated. "We've got to get all of us out of here!"

"Then I really *did* hear voices out at the cove that day!" Chet whispered, nudging both Hardys. "Probably these prisoners' cries!"

Frank nodded. "With Bedoya at work here, it would explain the *Atlantis* 'ghost screams'!"

Gomez, now conscious, was led in by the muscular man. The refugees cried out joyously:

"Gomez!"

"Luis! Pedro! *Amigos*—"

Gomez's greeting to his captive countrymen was cut short by a brutal slap from the thug. Reeling, Gomez was thrust next to the boys, who in whispers quickly established friendly terms with him.

"We owe you some apologies," Frank said, and briefly explained what they had learned.

Gomez was astonished upon hearing of the boys' visit to Baredo. "If only I had not become frightened and run away from you!" he muttered ruefully to Frank and Joe. "I was afraid to trust anybody before finding my missing friends."

The news of Colombo and Santilla's escape cheered Gomez. He had not been aware of the plot against Micro-Eye, nor of Bedoya's presence in Bayport. Gomez had learned of North's double-dealing while on the *Dorado* and also overheard Captain Burne speak of "the investigator, Fenton Hardy." The Huellan added that the search for his betrayed compatriots had finally led him to the cemetery at Oak Hollow and his capture.

The four stopped talking as Manuel Bedoya entered, followed by a heavy-set figure with his coat collar up. As the second man faced them, they gasped. Orrin North!

The magnate squinted balefully at the boys and Gomez. "You three have been a headache to us," he rasped angrily. "And you!" he strove over and shook his fist at Gomez. "You almost wrecked my 'refugee' business!"

"Business!" Joe retorted. "You mean kidnapping and treason!"

"Shut up!" North snapped his eyes blazing. "You Hardys will regret not co-operating with me. Too bad you would not heed the machete warning of Rodriguez and his friend."

"What's your motive in this spy game, North?" Frank asked coolly.

"Let's just say money."

Frank went on, "You pretended Gomez was a thief, provided the tomb hideout, plus the *Atlantis* for Posada's Footprints plot?"

"You catch on fast," North said mockingly. "The warning sign I put up here, and the ghost legend helped keep people away—but not you nosy kids. My pilot saw you snooping around the cove last week. I'll bet you copped that sea shell, too!"

North went on, boasting that leaving messages in the sea shells had been his idea. He pointed to the brawny thug. "Musco here swam the shells ashore."

"After you tricked these Huellans into giving names of underground friends," Joe accused him.

"Not me personally," North qualified, "but you've got the idea. Sometimes Bedoya had to be more—persuasive." He chuckled. "Nice system, eh? The shells were picked up, the names and other information hidden in clothes, and sent to Cayenne. How do you like my title: Orrin North, Liberator of the Huellas?"

Gomez's eyes blazed and he kicked at the magnate. "You dog!"

North stepped back, laughing raucously. He turned to Bedoya. "Manuel, I'm not hanging around here any longer than I have to. Everything ready for this morning?"

"Everything—if the *Northerly* is."

"It's shipshape." North rubbed his hands and said

to the boys, "Too bad you'll miss seeing us pull off our big job today. Manuel, they're all yours!" he added, and left.

Chet nervously watched as Bedoya leaned against the desk and fingered the riding crop.

Frank glanced up at a clock on the wall. Four A.M.! He decided to take the offensive.

"So Posada sneaked you in here via the *Capricorn* to get the Micro-Eye camera!" he said.

"Yes," Bedoya said, cracking the whip against the desk. Chet jumped.

The master spy continued, "I failed to learn from Miss Hardy on shipboard of your father's whereabouts, but I understand he is far from here, unfortunately for you!"

"You think you're going to break into Micro-Eye?" Joe taunted. "You don't have a chance!"

"I think we have a perfect chance," Bedoya countered blandly. He laughed.

Frank suddenly recalled Al, the spy, he had seen at the tomb meeting.

"We know you have an inside man," the young detective spoke up. "How did he get clearance as a guard?"

"Oh, but Al Raker's not a guard," Bedoya said, raising his brows. "He's a laundryman."

"A laundryman!"

"Of course!" Joe burst out. "The man I thought I recognized at Corporated Laundries! And I saw North in there—probably leaving a message!"

"Corporated Laundries!" Frank exclaimed. "So that's how Raker took photos inside the plant. But the maintenance building is isolated—where did Raker suddenly get a guard's uniform?"

Bedoya cracked the riding crop again, close to Frank's face. "You are very inquisitive." He smiled. "But I can afford to tell you."

The Huellan reached into a foot locker and pulled out a white work outfit. Stitched over one of the jacket pockets in red was the word "Corporated."

"Simple," he began. "Raker rides with Gale—also one of our men—in the truck to Micro-Eye. Raker sits in the back with the clean laundry. They are admitted by the gate guards. Then"—the chief spy grinned—"comes our little miracle."

Bedoya quickly turned the white jacket and trousers inside out. The boys gasped. They were identical to a Micro-Eye guard's uniform!

"The rest is easy," Bedoya continued. "Raker dons a moustache and forged badge, then he is let out at the maintenance building by Gale. Next, he walks to the main plant. Dykeman's guard-shifting plan helped—Raker goes about unsuspected."

"And with a miniature camera!" Joe cut in.

"Correct. Raker then returns to the maintenance building and Gale sneaks him back into the truck, where he once more reverses the uniform."

"But," Frank interrupted, "the gate has logged in *two* laundry employees in the truck. If Gale handles the laundry alone, wouldn't any guards watching be suspicious?"

"Gale doesn't work alone," Bedoya said smugly. "Since our laundrymen collect and deliver regularly at the maintenance building, the gate guards do not inspect the bundles."

"Inside one of which is another spy!" Joe finished. "He takes Raker's place until he gets back!"

"Ingenious, no?" Bedoya boasted. "Our third man comes in as 'clean' laundry and leaves in a pickup bundle. But today that bundle will leave with the satellite camera."

"Then why did you have Valdez try to cut through the fence that day?" Frank asked. "He didn't have a chance of getting in."

"Of course not," Bedoya agreed. "But it helped to make Dykeman think we were working from outside."

Frank pressed further. "And you used the luggage—and clothing—of innocent travellers to smuggle out the films and stolen data to Cayenne?"

"Correct," Bedoya affirmed. He admitted that Valdez had broken into travel agencies and obtained names of tourists flying to Cayenne.

Their agents at Corporated Laundries would wait for the travellers to leave dry cleaning there, the Huellan added. The Micro-Eye secrets were then cleverly sewn into some of the garments which the customer indicated he would take on the trip. In certain cases Valdez would have to risk entering the person's home to make sure the information *was* in the suitcase.

"And what happened to Raymond Martin?" Joe demanded.

"Oh, we have him safely tucked away." Bedoya would explain no further. Just then Musco whispered something in his ear. Leaving two armed thugs with the boys, the men left the compartment.

Frank, Joe, and Chet looked around for some means of escape. Their heads throbbed with pain. Gomez and the refugees slumped into dejected silence.

Suddenly clanking sounds from below and the gurgle of rushing water aroused the four prisoners. Frank again looked at the clock.

"Six-thirty!" he thought. "We *have* to get free!"

At that moment Bedoya re-entered with Musco. The boys and Gomez were unhandcuffed and pushed through the door towards a companionway.

"And now, we must part," Bedoya said jeeringly.

The Hardys, Chet, and Gomez were jostled down the rusted stairs. Musco, Rodriguez, and Bedoya followed closely. The sound of rushing water became louder. The group came to a halt outside a watertight door.

"I would have enjoyed testing your endurance at greater length," said the spy leader. "But time is short. All right, Musco!"

Musco threw open the steel door to the thundering din of gushing water. It was a dark aft compartment flooding from gashes in the hull!

"You'll never get away with this!" Frank shouted as loudly as he could.

But the next instant the boys and Gomez were thrust savagely into the turbulent chamber. Torrents of ice-cold sea water enveloped them as Bedoya's mocking voice rang out. "If you *are* found, it will appear as an accident. Remember—this is a ghost ship!"

His laughter reverberated. Then the heavy door swung shut and clinked. The icy water rose higher and higher, swirling about the foursome.

· 20 ·

Countdown

THE Hardys, Chet, and Gomez floundered in the darkness, trying to keep their heads above the rising water. They clawed around, groping blindly for a way out.

"This whole stern section must be submerged!" Frank realized.

The Hardys tried yanking at the steel door, but it would not budge. By now, none of them could stand. "I—I can't stay up much longer!" Chet gasped. As a furry rodent brushed his cheek, he choked on a mouthful of salt water.

Frank said, "Try to find out where the water's coming in! It's our only way out!"

The three dived again and again, desperately seeking a breach in the hull large enough for them to squeeze through. Their breathing grew laboured.

Gomez groaned. "It is no use! The openings are too small!"

"Keep looking!"

Joe, bursting above water, touched the overhead with his hand. There was almost no room left!

Then suddenly Frank felt a strong pressure against his feet. He plunged beneath the surface, fingering the bulkhead. An inrushing stream of water led him to a jagged hole about two feet high and a foot wide. Frank shot above.

"I've found the opening!" he shouted. "But we'll have to widen it!"

Joe and Chet wrenched loose a section of rusted pipe near the overhead and swam towards Frank's voice. "Here!"

With not a second to lose, the two boys dived and battered at the side of the opening. As they came up for air, Joe gasped, "We can't get enough force behind the pipe!"

Desperate, the four prisoners submerged again, each gripping the pipe. They pushed it against one end of the gash and tried to bend out the edge. Suddenly, to their amazement, the lever began to jockey with new force.

Someone on the outside was trying to help them!

The opening grew wider!

The boys felt as if their lungs would burst, but finally Gomez wriggled through, then Joe. He pulled Chet outside, and Frank followed.

When they broke the sunlit surface of Cobblewave Cove, the four drew in long, shuddering gulps of air. Utterly exhausted, they floated to a large hump-shaped rock and collapsed on to it.

Who had been their rescuer? Frank sat up.

"Fellows, look!" From the shadow of the *Atlantis*, somebody was swimming towards them! As the figure neared the rock, the Hardys cried out in astonishment:

"Dad!"

"Frank! Joe!"

Fenton Hardy grasped his sons' hands and climbed up. He wore old, torn clothes.

"Dad! How?— Where?—"

The well-built, keen-eyed detective was equally amazed at seeing his sons. Catching his breath, he explained, "I spotted Orrin North's yacht out here an hour ago from a motorboat I'd rented, and swam to the *Atlantis*. Are you all right?"

"Barely," Chet said, with a weak smile.

Gomez was quickly introduced, then Mr Hardy continued his story. Upon hearing men's voices from the wrecked freighter, he had dived near the stern. "When I saw the pipe coming through the hole, I knew someone was trapped, so I pitched in, not dreaming it was you at the other end!"

"You saved our lives!" Frank said. "But, Dad—you haven't been away? You've been in Bayport?"

"Yes, in order to watch North's activities. But tell me what you're doing here."

The boys tersely recounted their involvement with Micro-Eye, and explained Bedoya's imminent plot to steal the camera.

"At eight o'clock!" the detective repeated, shocked. "I saw the *Northerly* start up the coast a short while ago."

"With Bedoya and his men aboard!" Joe guessed. "Come on!"

Overcoming their fatigue, the five swam to shore. They raced across the beach, through the pine barrens, and up a dirt road.

Fenton Hardy looked at his waterproof watch. "It's almost eight now!"

Frank urged, "Let's flag the first car!"

Gomez, concerned for his imprisoned friends, was

reluctant to leave. "You wait here," Mr Hardy said. "We'll notify the Coast Guard and have them send a boat to the *Atlantis*."

"*Gracias!*"

A saloon approached, and the boys signalled frantically. The car stopped, and the Hardys and Chet jumped in.

"Micro-Eye Industries! Quick! Emergency!"

The young driver recognized the Hardys, and though puzzled at their bedraggled appearance, reacted instantly. "You bet!"

The saloon shot north along the coast. It was now ten past eight! Reaching town, the driver sped up a boulevard leading directly to the Micro-Eye plant. They heard sirens wailing. Eight-fifteen!

As the plant came into view, they gasped. Billowing smoke almost obscured the buildings. Squad cars idled along both kerbs. Policemen and armed plant guards seemed to be everywhere.

"Bedoya's smoke bombs!" Frank exclaimed. He directed the driver to stop at the main gate, as Joe yelled, "There goes the laundry truck!"

The brown vehicle was just turning the corner at the far end of the block!

"They've stolen the camera!" Joe cried out.

"Chet," Mr Hardy snapped, "find Mr Dykeman! Have him call the Coast Guard!"

"Yes, Mr Hardy."

As Chet hopped out, the detective addressed the driver. "We need to borrow this car. Will you trust us with it?"

"Sure thing!"

The young man alighted and Frank slipped behind the wheel. He sped off, heading directly for the waterfront. As they neared Bay Street, the Hardys saw the laundry truck ahead. It swerved round a corner. Frank followed just in time to see a large white bundle being tossed from the rear of the truck. It landed in an empty yard!

"The camera!" Joe cried out.

"This may be a trick!" his father argued.

Frank had already screeched to the kerb. Joe sprinted over and tore open the bundle. Empty!

In a flash he was back in the car, and Frank made for the boathouse area. He braked to a halt at the *Northerly*'s dock. The yacht was nearing the mouth of Barmet Bay.

"They've made the pickup!" Joe cried out. "Let's get the *Sleuth*!"

The boys and their father leaped out and started for the Hardy boathouse. Suddenly, from behind a green car parked nearby, two figures rushed towards them. The hulking Walton, and behind him Greber, wielding a machete!

The huge man lunged for Mr Hardy, but the detective side-stepped nimbly and jarred him to the ground with an uppercut. Frank and Joe tackled Greber. Two punches to the midriff sent the machete flying and he sank to his knees.

"Leave them for the police!" Mr Hardy said.

He and his sons rushed into their boathouse and boarded the *Sleuth*, with Frank at the wheel. He sped across the bay. The yacht had already reached the open sea.

"They're going to transfer the camera to another boat!" Joe shouted, recalling the spies' planned "off-shore pickup" by "41."

"Probably in international waters!" the investigator guessed as the *Sleuth* streaked from the bay.

The *Northerly* now raced full speed ahead, some hundred yards to port. In the distance the pursuers saw a small, net-draped sailing vessel. The *Northerly* plied directly for it, cutting speed.

"A fishing trawler!" Mr Hardy exclaimed. "'41'!"

"I'll try to get between them!" Frank steered straight for the tip of the *Northerly*'s bow.

The yacht's pilot swung left to avert a collision. The manœuvre had worked! But as Frank looped back towards the yacht, the larger ship veered sharply, and came at the *Sleuth*. The Hardys could see Manuel Bedoya, enraged, shouting to the pilot, Decker.

Joe yelled at his brother, "Look out, they'll cut us in two!"

Frank was forced to turn aside, and the *Northerly* resumed course for the trawler. Suddenly there came a thunderous boom!

The Hardys looked south at a rising patch of smoke. Two sleek, grey cutters with forward guns were advancing at full steam.

"The Coast Guard!"

Instantly the trawler's motors chugged to life. It headed out to sea, away from the *Northerly*. Bedoya's frantic shouts could be heard.

"Stop! You cannot desert us! Wait!"

But already one of the cutters blocked the *Northerly*'s path, and a stern voice blared out:

"Heave to!"

The yacht throbbed to a halt. At the same instant, Bedoya darted to the rail and flung a bundle overboard.

"The camera! Frank, quick!"

The *Sleuth* shot to where the object splashed into the sea. Joe dived and grasped the sinking bundle. He brought it up and was helped aboard by his father. By this time the trawler was a speck on the horizon.

Meanwhile, six Coast Guard men had boarded the *Northerly* and ordered Decker to head back. Manuel Bedoya stood sullenly in the grip of two officers.

With a Coast Guard cutter on either side, the *Northerly* returned to Barmet Bay. The *Sleuth* kept close behind. Within an hour after docking, Bedoya and all his cohorts had been arrested, and the camera found intact in a waterproof bag.

Soon afterwards, a large jubilant group sat in the Hardy living-room, awaiting lunch. Aunt Gertrude was spellbound by the whole story.

Mr Dykeman arose from a chair. "Fenton," he said warmly, "words can't express what you, your sons, and Chet Morton have done for our government."

The boys beamed, then Joe remarked, "The great 'liberator,' Orrin North, is out of business for good, I guess."

"I should think so," Aunt Gertrude said tartly. "And to think that I actually was on board ship with Posada's head spy!"

Dykeman reported that the smoke bombs had caused little damage to Micro-Eye and no one had been injured. "But the confusion did allow the phony guard Raker to take the camera—supposedly to safety, then to knock out two plant guards before he put the camera in the truck.

"By the way, Pryce has been exonerated," the intelligence man said. "Raymond Martin was found half-starving but alive in a remote shack outside Cayenne. The two suitcase thieves were with him. They confessed to having left 'his skeleton' to fool any prowlers."

Captain Burne and the *Dorado* crew had been apprehended in South America. The boys were pleased to learn that Gomez and the Huellan refugees had been assured of homes and a new start in the United States.

"Let's hope the spies' failure puts a big dent in Posada's power," Frank said. "By the way—that fishing trawler—does it just get away?"

"I'm afraid so," Mr Hardy replied, "but empty-handed, at least. Authorities believe the vessel belongs to a large, anti-American country—and, as you and Joe suspected, that Posada did plan to trade the satellite camera for money and arms."

Mr Dykeman chuckled. "Not even I suspected your whereabouts, Fenton."

Chet was still puzzled by the theft of Iola's shopping bag. "I can explain that," Mr Dykeman said. "When your dry cleaning was left at Corporated Laundries, Bedoya's spies mistakenly sewed the film into your clothing. They confused Morton for Martin, so Valdez had to get them back."

"One more unsolved mystery," said Joe. "Those footprints under the window, both at our house and North's."

Mr Hardy burst into hearty laughter. "Remember, you weren't the only sleuths around here."

"Dad! They were *your* footprints?"

"Guilty." The detective's eyes twinkled. He added, "To crack this spy plot, it was important that *no one* knew I was in town." The "stolen" papers, he revealed, were part of a dossier on North which he had to pick up.

Joe gaped. "Well, if that doesn't beat everything!" Unknown to him, however, the Hardys would soon be challenged by an even more baffling case, *The Crisscross Shadow*.

"Anyway," Chet said, sighing and relishing the prospect of a titanic meal, "one thing's sure about this mystery. There was an awful lot afoot!"

The others laughed heartily.

The Hardy Boys® Mystery Stories
by Franklin W. Dixon

There are many exciting Hardy Boys Mysteries in Armada. Have you read these?

The Clue of the Screeching Owl (9)

A terrifying apparition haunts gloomy Black Hollow. Camping in the woods, the Hardy Boys face spinechilling danger . . .

Hunting for Hidden Gold (25)

Frank and Joe go to the Wild West in search of treasure. But a deadly trap awaits them among the abandoned gold mines . . .

The Outlaw's Silver (65)

The Hardys face one of their trickiest missions — to destroy a vicious spy ring. But first they must cross miles and miles of unknown, treacherous forest . . .

The Four-Headed Dragon (67)

What is the link between an eerie old mansion and a plan to sabotage an oil pipeline? Only the Hardy Boys can find out in time . . .

Armada

BLACK HARVEST

by Ann Cheetham

A chilling story of terror and suspense…

The west coast of Ireland seems a perfect place for a family holiday — until everything begins to go horribly wrong…

Colin becomes aware of a ghastly stench from the land — a smell of death and decay… Prill is haunted by a fearsome skeleton-woman, who crawls through her dreams in hideous tormnt… Baby Alison falls sick with a sinister illness…

And their cousin Oliver? In those stiflingly hot summer days, as some nameless evil from the past closes in on them, Oliver remains unnaturally, unnervingly calm…

Armada

CAPTAIN ARMADA

HI KIDS! I'VE GOT THE POWER TO BRING YOU FUN, ADVENTURE, AND EXCITEMENT!

Here are just a few of the best-selling titles that Armada has to offer:

- ☐ The Bytes Brothers Program a Problem *L. & F. McCoy* £1.25
- ☐ Biggles — Charter Pilot *Captain W.E. Johns* 95p
- ☐ Race Against Time *Carolyn Keene* 95p
- ☐ Black Harvest *Ann Cheetham* 95p
- ☐ A Spy at Mill Green *Alison Prince* 95p
- ☐ Pony Club Cup *Josephine Pullein-Thompson* 95p
- ☐ The Mansion of Secrets *Frances K. Judd* 95p
- ☐ The Voodoo Plot *Franklin W. Dixon* 95p
- ☐ The Haunted Valley *Ann Sheldon* 95p
- ☐ The Whizzkid's Handbook 3 *Peter Eldin* 95p
- ☐ Trials for the Chalet School *Elinor M. Brent-Dyer* 95p

Armadas are available in bookshops and newsagents, but can also be ordered by post.

HOW TO ORDER
ARMADA BOOKS, Cash Sales Dept., GPO Box 29, Douglas, Isle of Man. British Isles. Please send purchase price plus 15p per book (maximum postal charge £3·00). Customers outside the UK also send purchase price plus 15p per book. Cheque, postal or money order — no currency.

NAME (Block letters) ⎽⎽⎽⎽⎽⎽⎽⎽⎽⎽⎽⎽⎽⎽⎽⎽⎽⎽⎽⎽⎽⎽⎽⎽⎽⎽

ADDRESS ⎽⎽⎽⎽⎽⎽⎽⎽⎽⎽⎽⎽⎽⎽⎽⎽⎽⎽⎽⎽⎽⎽⎽⎽⎽⎽⎽⎽⎽⎽⎽⎽

⎽⎽

⎽⎽

While every effort is made to keep prices low, it is sometimes necessary to increase prices on short notice. Armada Books reserve the right to show new retail prices on covers which may differ from those previously advertised in the text or elsewhere.